SEDUCED BY A SCOUNDREL

The Spinster Society
Book 3

By Alyxandra Harvey

Dragonblade Publishing, Inc. is an imprint of Kathryn Le Veque Novels, Inc.
P.O. Box 23
Moreno Valley, CA 92556
ceo@dragonbladepublishing.com

Produced in the United States of America

First Edition May 2025
Trade Paperback Edition

ARE YOU SIGNED UP FOR DRAGONBLADE'S BLOG?

You'll get the latest news and information on exclusive giveaways, exclusive excerpts, coming releases, sales, free books, cover reveals and more.

Check out our complete list of authors, too!

No spam, no junk. That's a promise!

Sign Up Here

www.dragonbladepublishing.com

Dearest Reader;

Thank you for your support of a small press. At Dragonblade Publishing, we strive to bring you the highest quality Historical Romance from some of the best authors in the business. Without your support, there is no 'us', so we sincerely hope you adore these stories and find some new favorite authors along the way.

Happy Reading!

CEO, Dragonblade Publishing

Additional Dragonblade books by Author Alyxandra Harvey

The Spinster Society Series
The Scandalous Spinster (Book 1)
A Deal With the Devil (Book 2)
Seduced by a Scoundrel (Book 3)

The Dainty Devils Series
The Duchess Games (Book 1)
The Countess Caper (Book 2)
The Husband Heist (Book 3)

The Cinderella Society Series
How to Marry an Earl (Book 1)
How to Marry a Duke (Book 2)
How to Marry a Viscount (Book 3)

CHAPTER ONE

I F SYBIL TAUNTON had her way, she would have brought the entire building down until it was rubble.

Twice.

Three times, even.

Gentlemen's clubs, as untouchable and ubiquitous as they were, deserved much worse than that. They sheltered men who dallied with other people's lives with impunity. Viscounts, earls, marquesses. The dreaded dukes. Fortune hunters, rakehells.

Murderers.

She would have lit a match to every club on St. James Street, if she could.

That said, it was rather convenient to have most of her targets gathered in one place. As a member of the Spinster Society, Sybil often had occasion to take down the kind of unrepentant man who languished inside drinking port wine and gambling away their sister's or daughter's dowry. It certainly made it easier when she knew where to find them.

The club currently in question contained a betting book which Sybil wanted.

Needed.

Was absolutely going to claim for her own.

Naturally, women were not permitted inside the club.

Naturally, Sybil was not going to let that stop her.

The very idea.

She had not let storms or broken carriage wheels or being tossed into the Serpentine stop her. Nor being locked in the Marquess of Eastbourne's cellar with several other women and chained to the wall. She was the only one with the dubious distinction of being chained to the wall—*after* she had tried to strangle one of the guards.

That she had been caught at all still rankled.

The fact that the marquess was found guilty, imprisoned, and stripped of his title was a balm. And no less than he deserved.

But that was ages ago.

Tonight, she was back in Mayfair, with the wealthiest and most powerful men in her sights and quite ready to topple them like toy soldiers. It was long past midnight, edging closer toward dawn. They were thoroughly in their cups, which was helpful. She might have waited for morning, when fewer members congregated, but it would be easier for someone to notice her then.

And it was so much more fun this way.

A challenge.

Not to mention that she had decided on her current course of action approximately twelve seconds ago.

She was not technically on assignment. Lady Priya Langdon, founder of the Spinster Society and general Keeper of Secrets, had suggested she take some time to rest after her ordeal at the Eastbourne estate.

Rest was *boring*.

And therefore detrimental to the soul, surely.

By the second day sleeping in late and drinking tea and wandering around Hyde Park, she was ready to chew the pretty silk paper right off the walls. Footraces against Peony helped. Practicing with the swords and the daggers kept in Spinster House's converted ballroom was always invigorating.

But as much as she tried to exhaust herself, she fell into bed unable to sleep—or worse, unable to stop waking up in a sweat, the weight of the iron chain pressing into her ankle. The raw marks had mostly healed, though they left some scarring. Her ankle was perfectly functional. It was rather dramatic of her mind not to leave well enough alone.

And now here she was, a lady on St. James Street in the middle of the night. St. James was Not For Women. It was an unspoken decree handed down throughout Mayfair. It was a gentleman's arena.

All of London was a gentleman's arena.

England.

The bloody world.

She would have this betting book. She would steal the secrets of the most powerful men in Mayfair. Tonight.

Right now.

In her fashionable dress and pelisse, with no regard for propriety. Nor the weather, which had decided on a cold drizzle but threatened to turn to ice with a moment's notice. Extremely rude for early spring.

But a perfectly good reason to let a lady inside where it was warm and dry.

She was not exactly prepared. She could have dressed as a maid and slipped through the side entrance. Or as a man. She was improving in her application of false beards. She had picked up the trick of using spirit glue from an acrobat at Astley's Amphitheatre.

None of which was helpful at the moment.

Sybil had a mad plan that was no plan at all, and the ability to cause unholy havoc.

Perfect.

Play to your strengths, as her mother was fond of saying. Of course, she generally applied it to social or political maneuvers, but never mind.

Sybil slipped inside the hallowed halls, which appeared to be like any other room in Mayfair: crowded, stuffy with smells of perfumes and cheroot smoke, wine spilled, candles guttering out.

The mahogany wood panels were polished to a gleam, as were every pair of shoes in attendance. It was shiny, loud, extravagant.

There was a great deal of yelling coming from the room with the card tables—which she could not investigate beyond a glance, as the butler had planted himself in front of her with a sniff. "Courtesans must enter through the side door and be vetted."

As an earl's daughter—adopted daughter, technically—Sybil could have taken offense. Great offense. Or else she was supposed to pretend not to know what a courtesan was—even at the age of twenty-nine, having been born somewhere in the Seven Dials but brought up in Berkeley Square. She was supposed to pretend a lot of things.

"It's raining," she told the butler. "Drizzling, even. It's very uncomfortable."

He blinked at her.

She tilted her head. "I am sure you meant to offer a lady shelter in such inclement weather." She loved the weather, actually. She liked the cold bite of the wind, the threat of a storm. Another thing she was supposed to pretend not to like.

"This is not appropriate," the butler insisted, his voice squeaking slightly. He was very high in the instep—she could see that by the perfect press of his cravat, the furrow in his brow when he found a woman daring to infiltrate his domain. But he was also at a loss as to how to deal with a lady.

Also, he was very tall. She might not be able to take him in a fight.

On second thought, she could take most men of his kind in a fight. The element of surprise was *always* on her side.

New plan.

Did it count as a new plan if there was not one that preceded it?

A plan, then.

Because behind the butler with the flaring nostrils was the betting book. Leather-bound, opened on a table next to a cut crystal glass holding quills. The inkpot was gold and shaped like a lion.

And behind them both: Keir Montgomery, the Marquess Blackburn.

A man she could *not* take in a fight.

Well, a *fair* fight, anyway.

Sybil had no intention of playing fair. The odds were never even, the battlefield never forgiving. The enemy always had a pistol to her parasol. Parliament. The law. Social convention. She had learned that here in the glittering heart of posh London just as easily as she had in the Seven Dials rookery where she spent the first six years of her life.

Keir leaned against the wall near the staircase. His hair was too long as always, thick waves that touched his collar. He was too tall, too muscular, too imposing. *Handsome* was too plain a word for him. He was arresting. Interesting. Impossible to ignore.

More's the pity.

She had been trying for years. They had been the best of friends as children and then strangers, and now... something else. Indefinable. Uncomfortable. Unwise to the extreme.

He was immovable, even as footmen scurried past him to serve drinks, members shouted insults, stumbled drunkenly past him. He stood, still as an anchor unbothered by the crashing waves. Only a twitch to avoid the spill of port wine a duke's grandson sloshed dangerously near Keir's boot.

He looked up and noticed a younger man playing cards, red-faced and sweating. One of the other players sneered. "Collingwood," Keir called out, easily heard through the din. "I wouldn't."

Collingwood swallowed, hand dropping away from his pocket. Sybil imagined to be caught cheating was bad enough for the reputation, never mind by a man impersonating a mountain.

Keir was formidable.

She knew it for a fact, seeing as he was her neighbor and had been for as many years as she could remember. She also knew the frown he was shooting at her, as if he wondered where she'd come from and how soon it would be before she could be dispatched back there. She had grown rather fond of needling him.

It was so much more comfortable than having her feelings hurt.

It hardly *mattered* that he did not care for her enough to acknowledge her in Society. It made no difference to her. He was not the first to disdain her and would hardly be the last. She was not a fool. She knew she was not easy to be around, especially for a person who wanted calm and control as much as he did. He was a marquess, after all. Even if his mother did come from the Highlands and had generally refused to set a single toe south of Hadrian's Wall. Keir often wore the plaid kilt of her family, which had always enraged his father. But his father was a lout. A dead lout.

And still nothing had changed between them.

Keir was wearing his plaid right now, which was clearly the only reason she was briefly fixated on his knees, the flex of his calves. Even as he continued to scowl at her as though it were his duty. King and country, and all that.

She beamed her brightest and most obnoxious smile in his direction.

He paused.

Just for a brief moment. Those green eyes focused so intently on her that she felt an inexplicable tingle in her limbs. A shiver sneaking through her. Must be the cold, damp wind sneaking in the open door behind her.

Or the relief of finally *doing something* addling her wits.

Doing something utterly mad, to be clear.

But what better distraction than Lady Sybil Taunton launching herself at Lord Blackburn, who did not care for her but secretly could not resist her? Just as she could not resist him, more's the pity.

It would create just the right amount of fuss and bother were she to confront him. Also known as: massive. Nearly as massive as Keir's chest, which she refused to be distracted by. A chest was a chest. An arm was an arm.

Theoretically.

She knew the gentle strength of those arms, the gleam of that chest in the firelight looming over her.

Sybil nearly apologized to the butler for the oncoming storm but then he sniffed down at her. Her spine turned sharp, her smile a sword. He swallowed, recognizing danger even if he did not know the form it was about to take.

Keir also recognized it, pushing away from the wall a moment before Sybil caught his eye and opened her mouth to screech: "Lord Blackburn!"

The king himself could have marched through the club with an accompaniment of armed guards and a parade of trumpets and no one would have glanced at him. Ladies of Mayfair did not breach these walls.

Ladies of Mayfair did not screech.

Ladies of Mayfair did not enjoy themselves.

Well, down with the apple cart to that, as they said in the rookeries.

While everyone around them paused, cards in hand, glasses frozen partway to lips, Keir only raised an eyebrow at her. Expectant, mildly exasperated. As if he knew her well enough not to trust her.

Well, she *had* released that ferret into his townhouse. Accidentally.

Mostly accidentally.

Never mind that now. Sybil considered squeezing out a tear, maybe a winsome tremble of her lower lip, but discarded the idea almost immediately. She was a fine enough actress, but the men in this particular establishment knew her a little too well, even if only through word of mouth, or a casual acquaintance with her father. They knew she was not winsome, that she did not tremble. Not even when chained to a wall in a damp cellar. That part was not public knowledge, at least. It would have made going undercover so much more difficult.

And so she settled for the snap of temper, the stubborn, defiant tilt of the chin. "How dare you, my lord? After proposing to me."

Keir blinked at her once, nonplussed.

Their betrothal came as a surprise to him—and to everyone else. Especially as he had been courting Lady Violetta Pontefract. Sybil spared a twinge of regret, but as the two had not been seen together recently, not even promenading at Hyde Park (not that Sybil had been paying attention), it was likely all hearsay. Idle gossip.

She had never asked him.

And she never would.

Either way, the gossip she created tonight was not idle. It served the Spinster Society. The women of London. It had a purpose, vicious and just.

And it made Keir's right eyebrow twitch, which honestly was reward enough.

And it created just enough confusion and shouting, both complimentary and uncouth (very well, mostly uncouth, it had to be said), to allow Sybil to dart past the butler. She glowered up at Keir, trying not to look as though she were enjoying herself immensely. "And you spent the night carousing instead of coming to tell me yourself that you had spoken to my father?"

Both of his eyebrows rose now. Before he could comment and take her little melodrama apart at the seams, she added. "And with *courtesans?*" She did not know why she had decided to add that little tidbit.

Those brows snapped together.

She might have winced, if wincing would have helped. And if she was the sort to wince.

She was not.

And yet...

She had to act swiftly before her very impulsive quest unraveled entirely. She had only made it this far because Keir was waiting to see what she would do next, not because he was hesitant to act. Even she knew that.

In for a penny, in for a pound.

She wavered on her feet, somewhat theatrically. Pointedly. She thought it only fair to offer him a warning of her intent if she expected him to catch her.

He *would* catch her.

He didn't care for her and he was angry with her, but Keir would never let a woman crumple to the floor.

She held his gaze, green and piercing, and let herself wilt. Slowly.

Just in case.

Keir caught her up in his arms, and if it secretly thrilled her—if her stomach fluttered and her thighs went hot—no one had to know about it. Surely it had more to do with the fact that she was *doing* something again instead of lying about *resting*.

Only that.

It was Keir. The strength of him, the warmth he exuded like a fire on a winter's night. The smell of smoke and amber that clung to him.

It was always Keir.

Alas.

Not the point.

Do not nuzzle him, she ordered herself.

"Sybil Taunton, what are you up to?" She remained limp, eyes slitted open only enough to keep track of her surroundings. When she did not reply, he added, "Are you quite done?"

"Not just yet," she breathed, barely making a sound. "I'm sure I need fresh air."

A sigh rumbled through him. It tickled her nose, tucked up against his chest.

"Felicitations!" someone shouted at him. "I thought you were courting the Pontefract chit?"

"So did I," Keir grumbled at Sybil.

She reminded herself once more that she did not flinch. Certainly not now, when she was supposed to be swooning. She had always considered swooning to be dull business. Lounging about with all the structural integrity of cooked celery.

She could see the appeal now.

Just a little.

Keir was just so large and solid. He carried her as if she weighed nothing. She was not particularly short nor particularly slim. No one had ever picked her up like this.

It was inconvenient to discover she rather liked it.

"I don't think swooning ladies smirk," Keir pointed out, stalking down the hall.

"Wait," she murmured against his cravat. She wanted to burrow her nose right into his throat.

Clearly, *clearly* too much resting was bad for the disposition.

She knew the rules. They never discussed them, but, regardless, they both knew the rules.

"Now what?" he demanded.

"Just move to the left a little."

He shifted slightly. She snaked out to grab the betting book, tucking it in the folds of her dress. Then she closed her eyes properly for the few moments it took for him to carry her outside and resolved to enjoy it.

New experiences were important, after all.

CHAPTER TWO

I**T WAS STILL** raining.

Sybil didn't mind. She felt squirmy and breathless and so overheated that she half expected steam to rise off her as Keir set her down on her feet. The cold wind snaking around lampposts and between buildings was soothing.

"Mind explaining what that was about?" Keir asked, gravelly voice deceptively mild. His eyes pinned her in place, demanding. A tiny bit menacing. Rain misted on his kilt, making him more suited to standing over a fire in craggy mountains purple with heather.

She liked it.

Oh *no*. That would not do. Not here. Not now.

"Terribly sorry!" She sent him a sunny, carefree smile. "No time to chat!"

And then she turned tail and ran.

She did not consider retreat cowardly. Not in this case. It was merely sensible. Tactical, even. She could be cautious when the occasion warranted it, despite what her fellow Spinsters said. Keir outweighed her by several stones. His arms were thick enough to toss trees about like kindling. Certainly strong enough to keep her still while he pilfered the betting book back from her.

It was hers now. She'd pilfered it first.

The rain, cursed by so many, was exceedingly helpful tonight.

It silvered the air, blurred the edges as she darted out of reach and slipped between two carriages. A coachman yelled something unflattering at her when he was forced to pull on the reins. "Apologies!" she yelled back, mostly to the horse. Water splashed around her shoes.

She could feel Keir's presence at her back, even as she knew she had lost him. There were too many wheels and hooves and buildings between them now. She knew the laneways better than anyone, even though she had not depended on them for her survival in a great many years. Her nan had walked her through the rookeries every day, her thick gray shawl full of holes young Sybil had loved digging her fingers through, like a fishing net. Fishing nets were her favorite—they made her think of her father, who was away sailing the seas.

It was not far to run to Spinster House on the edge of Hyde Park, and running was so much more enjoyable than strolling. The betting book was safely tucked into her cape, in one of the many large pockets she had sewn into all of her clothing. Some attached at the waist, under her dresses, some hung from her stays. Most of her capes were riddled with them. They were very useful for pilfered books, but also weapons of every kind, from hatpins to daggers to the pouches of mysterious herbs Priya handed out to the Spinsters. A spinster, a wallflower who could not find a husband, was the perfect person to offer you an innocuous, harmless cup of tea.

More fool you, if you accepted it.

Spinster House had been home for some months now. The society operated from a grand house Priya had bought, located right next to hers. She had been more interested in having a second greenhouse at the time, but it wasn't long before she filled the place with women, from Emmeline and Matilda, who lived together in the master suite of rooms, and Peony, to ladies who found themselves hiding from fortune hunters and bored aristocrats looking for a plaything.

And Sybil, who was perfectly welcome at home, but was also

twenty-nine years old and preferred not to have to come up with excuses every time she came home in the middle of the night.

Which was frequently.

Perfectly normal for a debutante or fashionable lady who spent her time dancing until dawn in silk slippers—less ordinary for a spinster who had not been asked to dance in some time.

Pity, as Sybil was quite good at waltzing.

But she had no dowry, even though her father was an earl. And as she was technically a foundling, she did not bring acceptable bloodlines to a prospective husband's lineage. It had not bothered her in years. She was extraordinarily lucky. Her parents were better than anyone, and she would poison the tea of anyone who suggested otherwise. Her hazy origins did not bother her, and more importantly, nor did they bother her parents.

They *did* bother every earl, Marquess, or duke she had ever met. If not them, then it bothered their mothers. Grandmothers. *Someone* was always very bothered.

Keir, who had been her closest companion and accomplice until he turned sixteen, was bothered.

Spinster House glowed warmly with lamps lit at the windows, always ready to welcome a weary traveler. A spinster being chased by a street gang of ruffians. And a drunken duke. Together.

One time, that had happened.

But Priya had taken one look at the state of Sybil and had lamps lit every night hence.

Sybil ducked into the lilac trees, most of the leaves plucked by the cold wind. The garden was a brittle shadow, but still a useful one. Yew bushes and statues of Roman women wearing circlets of roses offered a certain shield from the casual glances of people passing by. Spinster House was starting to become known, whispered about behind fans and over teacups. They straddled that murky line between needing to be secret and needing to be available.

Best that the Spinsters came and went through side entrances and back doors, less able to be accounted for by unfriendly eyes.

Sybil let herself in through the kitchen, laying her cloak over a chair by the fire to drip into the flagstones. She snatched a pear from a bowl as she made her way upstairs. The house was like any other grand Mayfair townhouse: parlors, ballrooms, bedrooms, servant quarters.

But here the ballroom was reserved for throwing daggers and fencing and practicing other such useful skills as climbing and pugilism. There was also a large pool of heated water where Peony spent most of her nights. She popped out of the glass room that had been built around it now, dark hair still damp, wearing a thick dressing gown. "You're drenched," she said. "And smug. Where have you been?"

Sybil and Peony had become closer friends due to the fact that they both kept the oddest hours.

And got into the most trouble, truth be told.

"Aren't you supposed to be resting?" Peony added, falling into step with her.

"Blasphemer. I thought you were my friend."

Peony snorted. "I was your friend until you made me lose a wager with Matilda. I said you would not last a single hour on your regiment of rest. And then you went and lasted several days."

"Barely. And only under duress. And hey! You wagered against me?"

"I wagered with reason and logic."

Sybil could not really argue with that.

"Since you clearly were not resting *tonight*, what have you been doing instead?" Peony asked as they ducked between giant potted ferns. Given Priya's love of horticulture, there were plants everywhere. It was a veritable jungle. Even the ladies' necessity dripped with roses and lilies.

"I went for a walk." Sybil grinned.

"Mm-hmm. Where, exactly? The bottom of the Serpentine?"

"Not this time. I was on St. James."

Peony grimaced. "Much worse."

"Usually, yes." They climbed the stairs, the polished wood creaking pleasantly under their feet. "But this time I breached Fortingham's."

"You went *inside* a club?"

Sybil tried not to look as smug as she felt and failed miserably. "I went inside, caused a fuss, pretended to swoon, and then stole the betting book on my way out." She waved the book triumphantly. She had left the part about being carried around by Keir, about the heat radiating off him, the scent of wood smoke and soap. The way she knew exactly how his hands felt gripping her waist.

"You did not!" Peony exclaimed. "And without me!"

"They would have bolted the doors against us if they'd seen us together."

"True."

"And possibly constructed a makeshift drawbridge to raise."

"And lit the torches, found some pitchforks. Cowards."

They grinned at each other as Sybil plopped the book down on Priya's desk and scrawled a note to accompany it. Unsurprisingly, Priya's office was stuffed floor to rafters with plants. And also a large basket stocked with bandages, ointments, towels. Baskets were scattered throughout the house with all the necessary supplies. Sybil knew she would find a flask of whisky under the clean towels. She decided she was not that cold and settled for a towel to dry her hair. She had never minded the cold before her experience of being locked in the marquess's cellar. She still refused to mind it, but lately there was definitely an invisible line drawn between the normal chatter of her teeth and something else.

She did not care for it.

Whisky helped, but she did not care for that either.

"Anything good in here?" Peony asked, riffling through the betting book.

Glad for the distraction, Sybil shrugged. "I didn't really have time to have a proper look. But I am sure Priya can find something useful." Stealing it was the fun part. She left the rest to Priya.

They skimmed pages of handwriting going back over a year. It would take some time to sort through. Peony shook her head. "These two idiots bet *two thousand pounds* on whether or not the robin sitting on the sill of the bay window of the club would fly away to the east or the west."

"Those two are dukes."

"Still idiots. And the Earl of Bellingham wagered he could sleep with a viscount's daughter and not have to marry her."

"Miss Middlemarch." Sybil nodded. "She broke his nose. It's still crooked."

"Well done, Miss Middlemarch. Perhaps she would like to join the society."

"She is not exactly a spinster. She is exceedingly popular and received seventeen marriage proposals this Season alone."

"Ghastly."

Sybil nudged her friend fondly. "Rather the point of a Season."

Peony shuddered. "Dancing is enjoyable but completely ruined by men sweating on you and talking about the weather or explaining things to you which you already know."

"They sweat on you because they can't keep up with you. No one has your stamina."

"They can't keep up with *you*, either."

"Yes," Sybil admitted drily. "And it has not made me particularly popular, either."

"Thank goodness for that."

Her lack of dowry was the actual impediment. She could have galloped across a ballroom, swung from the chandelier, and trod on all of the ducal toes she wished, if only she had a large enough dowry. And it had driven her dancing instructor mad when she was a girl. The moment she picked up the steps, she was incapable of practicing them over and over again. What was the point when there were so many other things to do? He had prattled on about grace and elegance and perfection in one's skill, but she had stopped listening before he had even begun.

That had not endeared her to future dance partners either, dowry or no dowry.

"Well, I am certain that Priya will enjoy combing through this," Peony added.

"I'll be back tomorrow, or the next day," Sybil said.

"Are you not staying here? It's late, even for us."

She shook her head. She mostly lived at Spinster House, but it was her father's birthday this week and the only gift he ever asked for was for her to spend it at home. She would sooner saw off her foot than disappoint him. Or her mother. They had taken her in, dirty and hungry, and then proceeded to immediately turn feral in her defense. She would not repay that kindness by adding even more chaos than she generally did just by existing. Best not to bring evidence into their house when she could avoid it. The book would stay here, and she would go home.

In the cold rain, still pelting down from the sky and still threatening to turn to ice.

Still, she was quite pleased with herself and the night's work when she ducked down the laneway to the mews and the side door leading to the music room. Footmen lurked by the front door, waiting to open doors and take away wet clothes. The servant door led down to the kitchens and the storerooms, where there was always someone lingering, even at this hour. Sybil had long ago learned the trick of the music room door, as well as the lower left window, which she could unlock with a length of wire she kept in one of her many pockets. In a pinch, she could scale the trellis at the back of the house and pull herself over onto her bedroom balcony.

Which, apparently, was tonight's route.

Someone had latched all of the doors and windows extra tight against the storm. Lightning flashed on wet window panes, the bent heads of shriveled roses in the gardens. It was unseasonably cold and damp for this kind of subterfuge, to be honest. She was already soaked through and shivering. Her nose was numb.

She loved it.

To a point.

A good thing, too, as she could see a footman passing through the house, candle glowing as he moved from room to room. A scullery maid would be up soon to light the fires. And although no one would be particularly shocked to see her climb through a window, the arrangement worked best when everyone could ignore her comings and goings. That way, no one had to talk to her parents about it (mortifying at her age) and her parents did not have to ask her any questions.

As another birthday present, she would not embarrass her gentle, kind father by making him ask her not to climb through windows in the middle of the night. He would worry. Her mother, just as kind but decidedly less gentle, would not ask. She would demand. Possibly with a sharp implement in hand.

The rookeries had taught her how to survive, and the Spinsters had armed her, but her mother was the one who taught her to stand her ground. And she would not let the Marquess of Eastbourne and the days she spent in his cellar take that from her. The fact that she hesitated briefly, wanting to simply sail through the side door and find her warm, dry bed, made it imperative that she scale the trellis instead.

It made perfect sense.

In her head.

She would not give in to fear. Or cold. Or memories of a cellar that in the light of day were not that terrible: she had not been alone, and they had all been fed and generally left on their own. She was the only one chained to the wall.

Sybil pulled a long leather lace from her pocket and tied it around her waist, tucking her skirts and cloak into it so it would not trip her up. Her fingers were already cramping with cold and her breath misted briefly in the air above her when she exhaled. A minor setback. She stepped up onto the decorative pedestal she had dragged into position months ago for this very purpose. She used it to reach the trellis and haul herself up, climbing swiftly. She had practiced in the Spinster ballroom for many hours. Peony had constructed a kind of obstacle course with a wall for scaling, which she delighted in pushing the members through until they cried. Or tried to strangle her.

Sybil had not cried, but she *did* try to strangle her.

Three times.

But it was worth it. She could climb like a cat, sure footed and nimble, even in the middle of a wet and unpleasant night. She was a little out of breath as she pulled herself over the balcony wall. She had not quite mastered the trick of doing it gracefully, it had to be said. There was a considerable amount of flailing and cursing. Her arms ached and her ankle was sore, but she felt better as she pushed into her bedchamber. More like herself.

Not at all like someone whose chattering teeth were causing distress. She was made of sterner stuff than that. She had once fallen through the ice on the edge of the Serpentine in January.

This was nothing.

Her chamber was familiar, the coals died down to red hearts in the grate, the smell of candles and flowers in the air. Her trunk at the foot of the bed. A bowl of yellow lilies, because they were her favorite when she was seven and her father insisted they should always be on her writing desk.

Everything as it should be.

Except for the large man lurking in the shadows.

CHAPTER THREE

S YBIL TAUNTON THREW a crystal duck at his head.

Keir barely had time to turn his head before it collided with his skull.

No one threw things at a man who towered over every other person in London. Possibly England. Certainly *ladies* did not throw things at him. Not since his sister had grown out of such behavior.

Or would grow out of it soon, saints willing.

Later, when there was not considerable danger to his anatomy, he would be glad Sybil was still so fierce, especially when presented with a man in her bedchamber.

Possibly not his best decision.

But she had needled him.

She always needled him.

And he liked things simple and comfortable. Sybil was neither of those things. Not on a regular afternoon, and certainly not when she was publicly wreaking havoc on his carefully structured life in the middle of the night. They had a wordless agreement not to entangle each other. He tried to resist her and failed, regularly. But that was private. Something for them alone. A link when no other link could be forged.

The fact that he had been bored senseless at his club was neither here nor there. He had been bored senseless at home too.

There were far too many nights spent in his quiet study, listening to the fire pop and listening even harder for Sybil prowling about her house. Hoping for another glimpse of her.

Those secret moments, those glimpses, were the only bright flame in the monotony of his irreproachable life. Household ledgers, estate matters, Parliament, letters from finishing schools about his little sister's behavior, which was far from ladylike and *finished*. The voice of his father berating him for failing at his duties, for being too gentle. The fear that he would instead be too hard on her. A new finishing school, and then another one.

So when her mother's cousin asked him to watch out for her young son on his one night in London, Keir had agreed. London was not gentle with lordlings, especially if they were Scottish. Bravado followed brandy every time. Then came wagers and duels and all manner of idiocy.

Thus, the club.

And the reason why he had even been available as a target when the storm that was Sybil Taunton blew through the elegant columned doors.

His family had had a house next to her parents' for as long as he could remember. He had watched her wreak havoc, dragging boot boys, footmen, maids, and, once, the kitchen cat into mad plot after mad plot. He had been the one to reclaim that cat from the tree between their gardens. It had not been grateful.

Sybil was not the sort of woman he could ever consider marrying.

Even as he considered it every single day.

He had painstakingly built the wall between them, brick by brick, polite nod by polite nod. He might not be able to stop himself from watching her—the way one kept track of a storm while out at sea—or from wondering what she was doing and if she was safe, especially after that debacle at the Eastbourne estate. It was not public knowledge, but Keir had a habit of hearing every story that involved Sybil. Purely self-preservation. She might well blow his house down, as it was so near to hers.

That he had not been there to save her ate at his soul.

She seemed oblivious to the danger she hurled herself into on a regular basis. How she was not missing limbs was a wonder to him.

But the only reason Keir remained in the London townhouse that had belonged to his father was to catch a glimpse of Sybil. To know that she was alive in the world.

He hated London, hated his father's house. Mayfair. But when Sybil was there, even just the sound of her laugh over the garden wall, it was better. It was always better. He remembered sitting under a tree, nursing a bruise from his father's temper and listening to her laugh. The basket of plums she brought him one day, before her cheeks flamed red and she darted away.

He had eaten every single one of those plums. He still thought of her when he ate plums.

But that was a long time ago.

His current problem was that she had merrily informed every drunken gossip on St. James Street that he was courting her.

He was *not* courting her. He would know if he were courting her.

Although the headache brewing behind his left eye cast some doubt on the matter.

Lady Violetta would be shocked when word reached her, as it would any moment now. Gossip was like a stubborn vine, winding through Mayfair, strangling everything in its path. The fact that he was unofficially courting her would feed that vine until it grew thorns and poisonous berries.

All because Sybil did not think before she opened her mouth.

Anger intensified the headache. She had just burned his carefully ordered life to ashes at his feet.

It was surely anger he was feeling.

Not a strange thrum of excitement.

Neither emotion was remotely soothed by the fact that Sybil also apparently disdained front doors, along with rules and common sense. Instead, she climbed up the side of her house, dripping rain, wind lashing icy bites across her face. Her fingers must be numb.

She put herself in danger the way most people put themselves into carriages: nonchalantly, as a way to get from one place to another. Concern warred with anger. He could be desperate for a glimpse of her and also desperate to lock her in his bedroom for a month to keep her safe.

Mostly to keep her safe.

But tonight he was here to sort through the mess she had created, to take back the betting book she no doubt thought he had not seen her steal right out from under the butler's nose. He had no idea why she would want it. He barely had any understanding as to why it was such an honored custom in the first place, treated with more respect than it deserved.

But if Sybil wanted it, it could not be to reasonable purpose. However much she might have changed over the years, she could never have changed *that* much.

"Keir Montgomery." She scowled at him. "What the devil are you doing lurking about?"

And then she threw another crystal animal, this one a badger. Just for fun, he imagined, as he had yet to move from his chair. He caught it, set it down on the floor. "Why are *you* climbing up the side of your bloody house?"

"*You* did the same!" she pointed out.

"How do you reckon that?"

"You would never knock on a lady's front door so late at night. Certainly not *mine*."

She was right. And now he knew exactly how sturdy the trellis was—not nearly sturdy enough with the icy lash of the rain. How easy it would have been for her to slip and fall. To land badly. She might have lain there for hours before someone found her. Acid burned in his chest.

"I don't live here," he reminded her through his teeth instead of saying all of the other things he wanted to say. As usual. "Last I heard, you do. The front door is not a scandal for *you*." Not that he imagined for one moment that she cared about that.

"You are lucky no one saw you," she said. "I can't imagine you would care for the besmirching of your reputation."

"No, you are right about that. I would say there's been enough of that for one night." She winced at his dry tone. This was the longest conversation they had had in months. Years. When they collided in private corners, in carriages or by the garden wall, there was very little talking. "But I also do not relish the thought of being challenged to a duel by your father."

She raised her eyebrows, the fleeting guilt in her expression gone like smoke on the wind. "As you know perfectly well, my father is a kind, gentle soul. My mother, however, keeps pistols hidden in the houseplants and would shoot your leg clean off."

"Duly noted. Why did you climb through your window? Afraid she might shoot *you*?"

"Maybe."

She wasn't. Not even a little bit. He knew her too well, even now. "Sybil."

She crossed her arms. "I don't have to explain myself to you."

He stood slowly. "Oh, I think you do."

She was dripping into the carpet and shivering.

He did not care for that.

She shivered again, and this time something passed over her face. A shadow of something he suddenly felt the need to skewer with a sword. To defeat utterly. Such an expression was not for Miss Sybil Taunton. Not while he still had breath in his body.

"You're cold," he said, because he very much feared he might start growling at any moment. Howling.

This was what came of consorting with the likes of Sybil.

Everything was too wild, too untamed. His entire chest cavity contained the feral winds of the Highland crags, all gorse and heather and teeth.

She shrugged one shoulder. "I'll be fine. It's not that cold."

Except that she looked like she might crack. Like she was made of glass under the wet cloak and the tangled hair, the tip of her nose turning red.

Keir stalked to the grate and crouched in front of it, feeding coal into the fire basket until the sleeping embers caught. The flickering light caught on the firedogs, shaped like crouched terriers ready to spring into motion. When he stood again, Sybil was fumbling with the ties to her sodden cloak, fingers moving numbly. He cursed and nudged her hands aside with far more gentleness than his expression implied.

"I can do it." Her teeth clacked together.

He didn't reply, only swept her up in his arms, for the second time that night, and carried her to a chair near the fire, tucking her against his chest. She laid her cheek against him, fine tremors working through her. "This is very unseemly."

"I wasn't aware you knew what seemly *was*," he said, but he tightened his arms round her in direct contradiction to everything he knew about himself. *Unseemly* did not begin to cover it. This was Sybil. In his arms. *Fucking finally.* That was always the first thought, no matter if it had been mere moments or months: fucking finally.

"I know what *boring* is, Lord Blackburn," she returned, just as drily.

"Lord Blackburn, is it?" he asked, inwardly calming when hints of her usual nettlesome nature peeked through. "So formal. And here I thought we were betrothed."

She wrinkled her nose. "You're cross."

"I'm confused."

"Cross."

"I can be both."

"You have every right to be," she admitted. "I am warm now." She wriggled, and he very nearly did growl.

"Stay still." He did not release her even though he should. Her cheeks were still too pale. She was too perfectly soft against him. "Your lips are blue."

He was being careful, that was all.

"Oh." Her voice was small, nearly a sigh. If he wasn't mistaken, she nuzzled against him. It made him feel… *Never mind.* "You are very warm."

"Yes."

"It's nice."

She smelled like rain and strong tea, and it was also nice.

Very nice.

Too nice.

"I cannot marry you, Miss Taunton." He felt compelled to say it out loud. Like an ass.

A complete and absolute ass.

She rolled her eyes. "Obviously."

He paused, frowned. Then wondered why he was frowning. "Oh?"

"I didn't mean to cause you trouble."

He snorted.

"What's that supposed to mean?" she asked, offended.

"Sybil, you are the very definition of trouble."

Why had it sounded like a compliment, even to his own astounded ears? He was usually better at hiding his true feelings for her. He'd had years of practice, after all. It could not unravel because he was finally holding her to his chest, enveloped in the sweet-spicy rosemary scent of her hair, undistracted by her soft thighs or soft sighs or his own desperate need to devour her from head to toe.

"I suppose I am," she said, suddenly unbothered. "To someone like *you*, most definitely."

"Someone like me?" He scowled down at her. Her hair was the color of warm tea touched with gold. Singular. In the summer it was like honey. He imagined wrapping it around his fist. Often.

"Proper. Orderly. Stodgy."

It was his turn to be offended. She made him sound like a prig. Like he was a hundred years old.

She patted his arm, suddenly looking as though she were enjoying herself immensely. "Don't grimace so. You're very… lordly."

"Wonderful." It was not wonderful. He was more confused than ever—and more certain than ever that keeping his distance from Sybil remained the best course of action. The sane one. The only one. Hadn't that been beaten into him?

"Was this some ploy to get yourself married?" he asked. "I've heard of ladies doing creative things to that end, but this is a bit much. And unnecessary. I am sure some gentleman will offer for you. No need to fret."

Sybil tilted her head back to blink at him slowly.

And then she laughed.

Right in his face.

Something else he was not accustomed to ladies doing.

And still he did not let her go.

SYBIL LAUGHED BECAUSE her other choice was punching him right in his very fine nose.

Which was tempting.

But she had already rattled him today, and she knew Lord Blackburn did not care to be rattled.

Also, she was already in the wrong.

Just a little bit.

But why did he have to be so warm? And so comfortable for someone who looked as those he were carved from stone? Hulking. Intimidating.

Lovely to hide behind when the weather turned.

All true.

And just as tempting as punching him.

But Sybil did not hide. Not even from her own mistakes. Even when she really, really wanted to.

She had made the pact with herself a long time ago. She knew she was reckless and impulsive and hard to deal with. The least she could do was take responsibility for the mess she sometimes left behind. Especially as she had no intention of staying home and knitting when she could be out wreaking havoc—also known as pursuing justice—for the Spinster Society.

Even if she *liked* knitting.

And truly, she had properly put her foot in it this time. Violence probably would not help matters.

"Keir," she said, sounding like a governess about to lecture him on geography.

"Yes?"

"Not every woman wants to marry."

"All evidence to the contrary."

She snorted. "Aren't *you* the popular one, then. I am quite sure the bumblebees are swarming to you. It must be such a nuisance."

The tips of his ears went red. "I didn't mean it that way."

She shifted her position. This conversation was best had while she was standing on her feet, not curled in his lap like a kitten. Sliding free of all that warmth and the soft stirring of his breath on the top of her head was more difficult than it had any right to be. She knew where this led. Where this always led. But tonight, it would not help matters. "Thank you," she said with slightly stilted politeness. "It was kind of you to"—*Hold me against your chest? Smell so good?*—"build the fire."

He nodded, just as stiffly. Lord Blackburn once again. "What prompted tonight's madness?"

She could not tell him she had stolen the betting book. And for the Spinster Society, no less. He would disapprove. He already disapproved. It emanated off him like steam from a boiled kettle, now that she was no longer pressed against him.

Pity.

"Sybil?"

Why did she like it so much when she said her name? His voice went stern and soft all at once, and it was intriguing. Confusing.

Annoying.

It was annoying.

"Yes?"

"No need to contort yourself coming up with a story. I already know you stole the Fortingham betting book."

And he was perfectly willing to pre-emptively call her a liar, as well as a thief.

As she was both, she had no business feeling a twinge of… something. Something unpleasant. Some of the lovely warmth left her. This was how it always ended: ashes after a raging fire neither of them could control.

He only waited with that legendary patience, one eyebrow raised. So she raised hers back at him. "I'm not giving it back. You can't have it."

"I know that too."

That he had seen her take the book was one thing. But now he would demand to get it back, she would refuse, and it would go on and on. He might tell the club, which would cause trouble for the Spinsters. For her father, most assuredly.

Best to play it off as a prank.

Another nail in the coffin of the very idea of Sybil Taunton as a reasonable woman.

And Keir would have no problem believing her.

"It was only a lark," she said lightly. "A challenge." Half true. She waved her hand nonchalantly. "You know how it is."

He believed her. Immediately. She could see it in his face.

Of course he did. Why wouldn't he?

It was addlepated of her to feel disappointment.

"A lark," Keir repeated.

She kept her smile firmly in place. It was a skill honed through long practice. First as the girl plucked off the streets and raised by an earl, with every other family in Mayfair whispering behind their fans, waiting desperately to be amused if she failed at dancing or pianoforte or used the wrong fork at supper.

But she played her part.

And as a Spinster, she had played many more parts outside of London Society: wallflower, stern governess, companion. Forgettable.

But Sybil Taunton of Mayfair was flighty, unreliable, unpredictable. Another part.

Most of it perfectly true.

It was only her reasons, her *purpose* that remained secret from most people in her life. Priya and Peony and the other Spinsters were her sisters in ways they probably did not even understand. They actually *saw* her. And they did not turn away because she was too much, too little. Too *something*.

They didn't look at her the way Keir was looking at her. With polite displeasure.

And he had every right to that displeasure. Tonight, at least.

Her smile did not falter. Not even when he sighed.

"It's not just my life you used like a plaything. Lady Violetta will be affected."

Sybil bit her lip. "I know." She did not care for feeling guilty any more than she had cared for being locked in a cellar. At least this was much easier to fix. She sighed. "There's a ball tomorrow tonight. Tonight, I suppose, technically, as it's nearly dawn. I'll tell everyone then. Please apologize to Lady Violetta for me."

He watched her silently for a very long moment.

She fought the urge to shift from foot to foot, to squirm like a sailor under the eye of a disapproving captain.

And then he inclined his head and left.

Just like that.

Infuriating mountain of a man.

CHAPTER FOUR

"*SYBIL IPHIGENIA TAUNTON.*"

Sybil had only been asleep for a few hours when her bedroom door flew open with the sound and fury of a tempest. Or outright warfare.

Otherwise known as her mother.

The door smashed into the wall and bounced back. Sybil opened one bleary eye to find Lady Amandine Taunton, Countess Wentworth, bending over the bed like some vengeful spirit in a ghost story. She was not amused.

Sybil blinked. "Gah."

"Is that any way to treat your mother?"

"To be fair, you're very fearsome," Sybil said, somewhat ruining the effect with a yawn large enough to make her eyes water. "Good morning, *Maman.*"

"Don't you good morning me, young lady."

"I'm nearly thirty years old, Maman." She squinted and made a noise of protest as the sunlight threw itself at her. Violently, it had to be said. "Ouch."

In the bright morning light streaming between the curtains her mother had just unceremoniously yanked open, her bedroom looked the same as it always did, even if it felt different. Mint-green silk wallpaper patterned with roses, prints she had pulled from *La Belle Assemblee* as a young debutante, tassels on the cushions, an armoire painted with bluebells. It was soft, pretty. Not at all like a room that had been host to Keir Montgomery. He was too big for Queen Anne chairs, too proper for trellises and bedrooms in the middle of the night.

Except, apparently, he wasn't.

Her bedroom at Spinster House was filled with notes on the habits and schedules of fortune hunters and known reprobates, daggers, hatpins for poking nefarious men, and baskets of knitting.

"Sybil, are you listening to me?"

"Of course I am."

"You are a terrible child."

"Again, nearly thirty years old, Maman. Practically decrepit."

Her mother kissed her forehead, then pulled Sybil's hair. "Rotten."

"Just as you like me."

"Exactly so." She narrowed her eyes. "Usually. If you're decrepit, what am I?"

"More beautiful than anyone has any right to be."

"Hmph. Better."

Sybil kicked free of the coverlet. Her hair, still a strange shade between brown and blonde, fell into her face. She had used a tonic made of steeped tea leaves and walnut shells to make it mousier for her last assignment, and it had worked rather too well. At least it no longer had a green tint to it. "Maman, please tell me you brought tea. And rolls."

"You deserve celery salad."

Her mother detested celery. Sybil winced theatrically.

"A daughter does not keep secrets from her parents."

Sybil snorted, just as theatrically. "You climbed over a garden wall to elope with Father. And that was *after* you hid in a trunk to cross the Channel."

"That's different." As it happened, Amandine had brought in a tea tray but was busy drinking all of the tea. Probably out of spite. Sybil *adored* her mother. "Lady Cartwright cannot know that my own daughter is being courted by the Marquess Blackburn *before I do.*"

Oops. Sybil ought to have seen this coming. Lady Cartwright was her mother's nemesis. They smiled at each other at the dressmaker's, complimented each other at the Royal Art Exhibit, and spent every single moment in between plotting to outdo the other. It was exhausting for everyone but them. The Prince of Wales had less elaborate parties. In fact, he had once been forced to intervene.

"The marquess is not courting me," Sybil admitted.

Her mother went from annoyed to deeply affronted in a single moment. "And why the hell not?"

Sybil grinned. "English countesses don't say hell."

"*Merde.*"

"That either, I am sure. My governess was quite clear on the matter, though we all knew I would never be a countess." It would have been more useful if she had been allowed to practice her tree climbing or knot tying.

Amandine drew herself up, and though she barely reached most people's shoulder, she was no less terrifying for it. "Did he say that?"

"Who?"

"Blackburn. Did he imply you were not good enough for him?"

"Of course not."

Except that he had. A long time ago.

Sybil was the daughter of a sailor who did the best he could until the sea took him, and a mother who succumbed to a fever. When her nan also died, the rookeries had kept her alive until Amandine spotted her from her carriage window that cold winter's day. "Regardless, Maman, all of Mayfair says it regularly."

"*Salots.*" When Amandine reverted to her mother tongue, it was never a good sign. There were men in the highest ranks of the royal court who ran for cover at the thought. Amandine had survived the very real threat of the guillotine before being smuggled to England. Nothing scared her. "I thought they had stopped being so... *English.*"

"Only around you." Sybil hugged her fondly and used the opportunity to steal a raisin bun from the tray behind her. "It hardly signifies."

"Hmph."

"Truly, Maman. It's of no consequence." She had come to terms with it within the first month of being in this house, even if her parents flatly refused to, even now. Her mother would fight the devil himself. Her father just got that slightly bemused and sad look on his face when anyone dared disrespect her in his hearing. Then he promptly went behind their back, if it was a gentleman, and voted against their bills in Parliament and paid off their mistresses very handsomely to break with them somewhere public. Her mother began rumors about the pox and unsatisfying bed-sport skills.

She really did adore them both.

"It's all a misunderstanding," Sybil added. "I will clear it up tonight at the ball."

"Your father still will not let me host a party for him, not even for his birthday." Amandine was very close to pouting. "He turns sixty next year, and just see if he can stop me them. Not to mention that Lady Cartwright had those acrobats last week at her dinner. Not a single one of them fell on their heads or scattered spangles in the pudding."

"Most disobliging."

"I thought so." She narrowed one eye. "Are you quite certain he is not courting you? I should dearly love to plan a betrothal ball. We could release swans."

"Quite sure." The idea Keir considered courting someone like her was... well, laughable. "He is courting Lady Violetta. Unofficially, I think, but still." Enough that he had been concerned for her feelings and reputation straightaway. Which was very honorable. Proper.

Sybil's insistence on doing things that regularly threatened her reputation would make him cry daily.

"And swans are vicious to anyone but you, Maman."

Amandine sighed. "Pity. I like the Marquess."

"You like his muscular shoulders."

"*Certainement.* Have I taught you nothing, *ma puce?*"

Sybil's father, Charles Taunton, Lord Wentworth, was a kind, intelligent, and extremely distracted gentleman. And currently distracted enough by the new music sheets in his hand to blink at Sybil as though he did not recognize her. One more blink and his smile beamed from his handsome, dignified face. "Sybil! Did I know you were home, ferret?"

She kissed his cheek. "As you demanded it for your birthday, yes, you did."

"I'm sure I do not *demand.*" He winked at her over his coffee cup. "Your mother is trying to get me to eat cake for breakfast."

"My mother is going to make you parade around in a frock coat spangled with beetle wings next year while an opera singer serenades you and the Prince of Wales drinks all of our champagne."

"She wouldn't." He looked briefly queasy.

"She has already started collecting the beetles. And last year, she tried to hire a trained bear for *my* birthday, remember?"

"That sounds…"

"Inevitable. Lady Cartwright had acrobats at her dinner. And an alligator during the summer."

He snorted. "That was no alligator."

"It was the family dog wearing a costume," Amandine announced, marching into the breakfast room. "He chased a sausage and urinated on the vicar." She smiled sharply. "I am quite certain I can beat *that.* Hardly a challenge."

As the French Revolution had not daunted Amandine, Lady Cartwright and her gold-threaded wigs and incontinent family dog were unlikely to manage that particular feat. Sybil's father had once told her that when her mother got bored, she got sad. And as he could not abide his wife's unhappiness, he was perfectly content to fuel and finance all manner of feuds and falderal. It was rather sweet, really. Even if she did have to climb through holly while wearing wire wings made of real swan feathers once. They had weighed far more than one might imagine. And they did *not* smell nice. Sybil shuddered.

"You're thinking about the Christmas pantomime," her father said.

Amandine rolled her eyes. "Oh, you two. So dramatic."

"*You* are not the one who got trapped in a tree," Sybil pointed out. Covered in blood from the pinpricks of the holly bushes around the roots.

"You were fine. You loved climbing trees."

She did. She had at ten years old, and she still did even now. Only now she did not have to wear wings and a crown of lit candles while being poked by holly leaves.

"We almost set the church on fire." Sybil grinned.

Amandine shrugged and smiled back. "English churches ought to be made of sterner stuff, then. We barely singed the stones. It's hardly my fault they let trees grow so wild next to the building."

The earl had to replace two windows and buy new pews and gold candlesticks for the altar as an apology. His wife and daughter had made no apologies, as they were too busy chortling with laughter, tears running down their chins. Lord Wentworth had only smiled fondly and asked to see the rectory pianoforte. Sybil's angel wings were unsalvageable. Thankfully.

They still talked about that Christmas pantomime some sixteen years later.

Amandine accepted a plate of eggs and herbed potatoes with Brie wedges from a footman. "Thank you, Jean-Paul." Amandine did not care for the social rules that frowned upon thanking the household staff. And she despised English cheddar and would only eat Brie or Camembert brought from France. She maintained that even though her homeland tried to murder her, they still made the best cheese. And the best servants, even if most of them had lived very different lives in Paris. Cook, once known as Madame de Beauchamp, had danced at Versailles.

They were halfway through the meal when a knock sounded at the door. "Oh, never mind that, Papillon," a cheerful voice floated down the hall. "I know the way."

Papillon, seventy years old if he was a day, almost managed to outrun the young lady who burst into the breakfast room. He had been the one to help Sybil's mother run from the guillotine, but there were few who could outrun Lady Sophie Montgomery, sister to the Marquess Blackburn.

"Sophie!" Sybil hugged the younger girl. She refused to be either relieved or disappointed to see that her brother had not accompanied her. Not a surprise, as he never would have allowed her to gallop through the house in such a manner. "I did not know you were in Town."

Sophie rolled her eyes. "My brother wants to keep an eye on me."

Sybil grinned. "What did you do?"

"Hardly anything at all."

"Sit down and have some cake, Sophie," Amandine said. "I miss hearing about a good escapade. This one hardly ever makes the dowagers cry anymore." She made a face at Sybil.

Sybil had spent a week chained in a cellar. And was regularly on the run from spoiled and powerful firstborn sons, but she had learned to keep it from her parents. Her mother might enjoy a good story, but she worried when no one was around to stop Sybil. And her father would not be thrilled to know she had stolen from *his* club.

"She does not deserve cake," Keir said from the doorway. His tone was very hard, very sharp. But when he smiled at his sister, there was only fondness. Despite the crease of worry between his eyes. "Lady Wentworth, Lord Wentworth. Miss Taunton. You look... warm."

The last time she had seen him, she had a red nose and was shivering so much her teeth clacked. She absolutely would not call up the feeling of sitting on his thighs while the fire crackled.

Or wonder if he was remembering it too.

She met his eyes and felt the force of it sizzle down her spine.

"Everyone deserves cake on my birthday," her father said.

"Jean-Paul, bring the Marquess some coffee, *s'il-vous-plait.*"

"*Oui, madame.*"

Sybil found herself with the ridiculous urge to fidget when Keir sat across from her, taking up all of the space. All of the attention. All of the air. This was not how they occupied each others' lives. There were strict rules, however unspoken.

"How did you find me?" Sophie pouted. "I was gone barely three minutes."

"You always storm the Wentworth house when you've been sent down in disgrace," Keir said mildly.

"I was not."

"You put porridge in the headmistress's shoes. You were kicked out of the best finishing school in England."

"She deserved it," Sophie maintained with a sniff. "She called me a slattern."

Keir narrowed his eyes. "Pardon?" His voice could have frozen the Thames at midsummer.

"Oh, she *did* deserve it," Sybil said, just as cross. "Next time, use honey."

"Oh, that's brilliant," Sophie said.

Keir pinched the bridge of his nose. "Please don't. I will deal with the headmistress."

"Anyway, I only came to wish Lord Wentworth a happy birthday. It's only polite."

"You came because you knew there would be cake."

"*Your* cook won't make sweets," she said.

That sounded dire. A cook who would not make sweets was grounds for a riot, in Sybil's opinion.

And in her mother's, if the flash in her eyes was anything to judge. "Whyever not?"

"Cook says I'm getting fat."

"Cook is fired," Sybil muttered.

Oblivious, Keir continued, "And you came without a chaper-one."

Sophie rolled her eyes so empathically this time that they were in very great danger of falling out of her head and rolling across the embroidered tablecloth. "I don't need a chaperone to walk next door."

"In very great point of fact, you do. This is London," he pointed out before drinking from his cup as though it was not dwarfed entirely in his massive hand. "And you are you."

"Rude." She forked up an enormously large mouthful of cake in defiance.

"You are, yes."

"Keir!"

"Oh, I do miss this." Amandine smiled wistfully.

"Sybil can be my chaperone," Sophie declared. "She's… old. No offense."

"Decrepit," Sybil's mother agreed, smiling into her coffee.

Sybil was not sure who appeared more horrified at the suggestion: herself or Keir.

Keir.

Definitely Keir.

"Your brother thinks I am a bad influence." He was probably even now panicking over the idea of her teaching his sisters to swoon and steal and climb trellises. She ought to do it anyway. A girl needed hobbies. Not to mention, certain skills to survive.

And funny how he was perfectly able to make facial expressions when Sybil was around. Even if they only ranged from exasperated to horrified. The stoic Marquess no more.

"That's because you *are* a bad influence," Sophie returned cheerfully.

"Traitor. You should be nice to me. Who else do you think will sneak you out to meet your many beaux?" Whom she would research most thoroughly first. Girls of sixteen fell in love. And love was not logical.

The look Keir sent her way was thunderous. Stern. Very strict. Demanding of respect.

It had the opposite effect on Sybil. She very much wanted to break all of his rules just for the fun of it.

But not today. Not at her father's table. And not when she already owed Keir an apology for possibly ruining his courtship of Lady Violetta. At the very least, complicating it. Even thinking about it made the back of her throat ache.

"Now you've done it," Sophie muttered. "When he glowers like that, it's never good."

Sybil smiled, even if there *was* something about the clench of Keir's jaw that made her sad.

Just a little.

He was not actually made of stone, despite the width of his shoulders and the demands made upon him by his father. And Society. She wondered, for the first time, if he even knew that.

Another knock sounded at the front door.

"So many visitors today," Amandine said, smugly pleased. "And before noon! Your birthday is always such an occasion. I do wish you'd let me order fireworks."

"You already did so regardless of the fact that I said no." Charles smiled at his wife.

"True."

Papillon led Lord Bentley through the doorway. He was very tall, his shirt points starched into tiny knives aimed at his eyeballs. Sybil did not understand fashion sometimes. Keir's shirt points were always so normal, his cravat simple and elegant.

"Wentworth, regards of the day."

"Thank you, Bentley."

"I'm afraid I've come with some bad news from the club." Bentley was already turning red with affront. "Which your daughter purportedly entered last night."

All eyes turned to Sybil. She smiled. She had learned to smile at anything. Everything.

"Did she, now?" Charles asked, unperturbed. "That's hardly bad news."

"It was raining quite dismally, Papa," she explained. She could not look at Keir.

"I am quite sure no one would begrudge you shelter," Amandine said, thorns poking through the roses. "Isn't that so?"

"Of course, my dear. Bentley," Charles added, "I know you recognize my wife."

"Apologies. Lady Wentworth, you look lovely as always."

"*Merci*," Amandine replied, twinkling. She always twinkled and spoke French to the aristocrats who disdained her home country. "Have we been introduced?"

She also pretended not to remember them.

It infuriated them.

And if they insulted her daughter, she eviscerated them.

"Lord Bentley." He bowed stiffly, introducing himself needlessly. Sybil bit the inside of her cheek to keep from laughing. He frowned at her. "Did you take anything last night?"

She widened her eyes. "Pardon me?" She had been accused of stealing more times than she could count. Whenever anything went missing, the *ton* whispered about ill breeding. Every tea party until she was eleven years old and refused to attend involved hiding the silverware from her, all while gently born aristocratic girls got away with everything by blaming her.

Sybil did not bother pointing out that she only stole from them *after* they accused her. For justice. Vengeance. A lark.

If she did not take them seriously, they could not hurt her.

"Yes, Bentley," her father said. "What exactly are you accusing my daughter of?" He sounded bemused, confused. Also furious, if you knew how to read the way he drummed his thumb on the table, waiting for a response.

"Fortingham's betting book is missing," Lord Bentley announced in resounding tones best suited for the stage.

"Is that all?" Amandine waved her hand, dismissing the subject entirely. "How... dull."

Lord Bentley drew himself up. "The gentlemen in that book would consider it a breach of honor, Lady Wentworth."

"Then those gentlemen clearly need to find themselves a hobby. Something soothing, like flower arranging."

Lord Bentley was as visibly confused as Sybil's father, and as furious, but for obviously different reasons. Her parents had that effect on people when they joined forces, which was often. "The only other shocking event of the night was Miss Taunton crossing the threshold of a gentlemen's club. Badly done."

"Do not reprimand my daughter," Charles said, suddenly looking a lot less distracted.

Keir did not say a single word, but he rose slowly to his feet. Lord Bentley glanced up at him. Up and up and up.

Sybil fluttered her eyelashes. She felt like an absolute idiot, but it always worked on men such as Lord Bentley. "What *is* a betting book, exactly?"

Keir glanced at her. Just once. She fluttered her eyelashes harder, at him this time.

He raised an eyebrow.

"A betting book... is a ledger. It's no concern for a lady," Bentley said.

"What does it look like?"

"Why does that matter?"

"How can one help you find it if one does not know what to look for? There are hundreds of books in London. Thousands. It must be very vexing to have misplaced it."

"It was not misplaced."

"Well, as I am a woman and it is not my concern, as you say, then I am sure I cannot help you." She kept her smile in place. "Regrettably."

"This is a serious matter, Wentworth," Bentley insisted. "Homes will be searched."

Interesting. Sybil filed that away for a later discussion with Priya. As well as Bentley's agitation, though she put that down to privilege and entitlement. "You are welcome to search my chambers," she offered.

"The hell he is," Keir snapped, before anyone else could reply. Amandine smiled at him slowly. "Bentley, you're leaving," he added. "Now."

"Blackburn, it's your club too."

"And I could not care less about the betting book."

"You were there! You carried her out!"

"I swooned, was all," Sybil explained. "It was very *womanly* of me. So feminine, wouldn't you say? Lord Blackburn was very courteous."

Keir's expression hardened, sharpened. Phantom swords and claymores clashed. A cannonball whistled through the air. "Be very careful, Bentley."

Lord Bentley swallowed.

"Yes, you do seem overwrought," Amandine said. "Men can be so emotional."

Lord Bentley was not just emotional—he was utterly flummoxed. He glanced from Charles's shocked and sad expression—which he did not yet know meant that his next session in Parliament would be contentious—to Amandine, who looked like the cat who had caught the hapless mouse who thought he had free run of the larder. Keir was a tower of quiet menace. Sybil sat as demure as a debutante.

"I'll walk you out, Bentley," Keir said. It was not a suggestion. "Come along, Sophie," he added.

Sophie stood up, eyes round. Breakfast was probably seldom so exciting at school, porridge in the shoes notwithstanding. "See you soon, Sybil."

Keir did not look pleased. He did not look anything at all, in fact. His face was stone again.

"Of course," Sybil said, lifting her chin, feeling too many things and unable to name a single one. "Call anytime, Sophie."

Her mother turned to Sybil and smiled her mysterious smile, the one her father called her *French smile*. The smug one that strongly suggested she knew more than you and always would.

"The courtship was just a misunderstanding, you say?"

CHAPTER FIVE

ONLY ONCE HER father felt thoroughly spoiled as well as exhausted by being the center of attention did Sybil excuse herself. She was itching to see if Priya had made any progress with the betting book. To see if her impulsive actions were worth the humiliation she had set herself up for.

Breakfast had not been reassuring on that end.

The Willoughby ball was one of the most anticipated events of the winter. Lord Willoughby could not compete with her mother, of course, who filled the garden with fire eaters, or Lady Cartwright, who had once suspended delicate nets of rose petals from the ceiling to release onto the dancers below during a waltz. But Lord Willoughby had a chef who inspired duels over a roasted duck recipe, as well as a wine cellar that princes wept over.

Everyone would be there. Invitations were fought over, stolen from the best of friends, bought with gifts that arrived well before the Season.

The gossips would swarm.

And Sybil was going to offer herself up as the main course.

She groaned under her breath and quickened her step. She had decided not to wait for the carriage. The air was crisp, and the faintest trace of hoarfrost glittered on windows and lamp-posts. She was impatient to be away, to be doing *something*.

Something that did not involve humiliating herself.

Walking all the way to Spinster House was not much, but it was a start. She caught the occasional glance thrown her way, but whether it was because of the growing rumors or because she was marching like a soldier to battle was unclear.

It felt familiar.

It felt very much like someone was following her.

She did not alter her pace or turn her head, though she dearly wanted to. She knew better than that. Just as she did not turn onto the street where Spinster House waited. Instead, she walked past it, chose the next turn, and went into Hyde Park. After the last few months, the Spinsters had set up new ways into the house.

Just in case.

She was not the first to be followed and was unlikely to be the last.

The back of her neck prickled. She wanted to spin on her heel and throw a punch. Alas, even a covert glance showed nothing out of the ordinary. She could be imagining it. Either way, if there *was* someone out there, he was not close enough for her to do any damage.

Which was no fun at all.

She turned onto a path grown over with yews and juniper, still green despite the weather. Sybil had a sneaking suspicion that Priya had planted the blackberry brambles herself to add cover all the year round. A few steps back and Sybil would be at the gate to the house's back garden, also hung with holly to discourage approach.

Instead, she waited for a moment, and another, tucked safely in the copse, the edge of Hyde Park stretched out before her. Yellowed fields glittered under the weak sunshine with meandering paths where couples walked arm in arm, nannies pushed prams, children ran with their dogs. No one lurked with obvious menace. Nor even with stealthy menace, if she was truthful.

No one was following her. She was being a goose. Her brain

was quite sure of that. The prickles at the back of her neck took a little longer to be convinced.

With a shake of her head, Sybil pushed through the greenery and used her key to unlock the secret garden gate. She passed the greenhouses, stuffed with orchids and lemon trees and more plants than she could ever hope to name. The back door was unlocked, though a footman appeared the moment she stepped inside. Sybil grinned at him. "At ease, soldier."

Footman was a bit of a misnomer. For one thing, most footmen wore wigs or livery. They did not carry knives about their person. But at Spinster House, things were different.

Naturally.

The lady of the house knew more than a dozen plants to poison your tea. The ballroom was more of an obstacle course. The scullery maid had once stolen a pet bear she did not think was being treated well enough. And Pierce Gallagher, formerly of the Royal Navy and Priya's paramour, had infiltrated the household staff with his own men to guard the house.

"Miss Taunton." The footman nodded to her. "Lady Priya is in the family parlor."

"She's expecting me, is she?"

"Sybil, is that you?" Peony called down from the staircase landing. "Hurry up!"

Sybil tossed her cloak over a chair and went to join her friend.

"Why did you come in the back way?" Peony asked when Sybil joined her.

"Just keeping in practice," Sybil said. If she admitted she thought she was being followed when she was not, someone would tell her to rest more, and then she would have to bite them. This was safer all around.

They went straight to the parlor reserved for the Spinsters. There were no stuffy rules of decorum here, often no shoes, sometimes only dressing gowns. There was tea, baskets of pastries, whisky on the sideboard. This was where they rested, where they planned and plotted.

Priya sat by the window, her dark, glossy hair pinned in a simple twist at her nape and the gold bangles she always wore gleaming at her wrists. A bronze statue of an elephant-headed man sat behind her with his jovial expression. Someone had left a plate of boiled sweets in front of him.

Matilda and Emmeline were curled close together on the settee. Matilda had long kicked off her shoes, which were always the very height of fashion and the very devil to wear. Peony sat on the floor like the hoyden she was, and Sybil would have joined her, but she had worn a proper gown in deference to her father's birthday and it was too narrow at the hem. She ducked under a fern that had no business being as big as it was and sat in a gold velvet chair with a cushion shaped like a lemon instead. "Good morning, all."

Priya glanced up from the betting book. "Do I need to tell you that you were too reckless and there might be consequences?"

Sybil snorted. "As I have to attend the Willoughby ball tonight in order to eat crow, no. No, you don't."

"Oh good, because I really, *really* wanted to get my hands on this book."

They exchanged a grin.

"Have cake with that crow," Priya added. "You deserve it."

"You're not going to tell me I should have been resting?"

"I dislike stating the obvious."

"I've never been inside a gentlemen's club," Matilda said. "What was it like?"

"It smelled of port and pipe smoke and honestly was not worth the fuss."

"I thought as much."

"Lord Bentley is already in high dudgeon over the theft. He all but accused me over my father's breakfast plate."

"That's remarkably rude," Matilda said, blinking.

"He was rather overset," Sybil said. "And I admit, perhaps, it was not my best move to be so obviously seen the same night the book mysteriously went missing." She shrugged. "Too late now."

"As your father is the soul of kindness, I hope your mother made him cry. Just a little."

"She forced him to introduce himself and will no doubt continue to exact her revenge." Sybil grinned. "The Courteous Cut. Death by a thousand social paper cuts."

Sybil thought of Keir, of the way he had risen from his chair, all coiled violence. Not at all the stoic marquess who barely looked at her when there were others around. The man who exemplified duty and responsibility, nonchalant even at the point of a sword. He had become that sword between one blink and the next.

Cold, sharp. Menacing.

Delicious.

It surely said something distasteful about Sybil's character that she thought so.

Ah well. She could add it to her already long list of flaws.

"Is Bentley in the book? Protecting himself, is he?" she asked.

"Yes, if I recall," Priya said. "But nothing out of the ordinary that I could see. Just the usual peccadilloes. I expect his pride is stinging more than anything."

"And why must you eat crow?" Emmeline asked over her cup of coffee. It was thick and strong, and no one else could even abide a single sip. She had been banned from making it for the rest of the household.

Sybil wrinkled her nose. "I may have announced to all and sundry that Lord Blackburn was courting me."

"But he is courting Lady Violetta Pontefract," Matilda said.

"Yes." Not even Sybil's closest friends knew what happened between her and Keir when they could not help themselves.

"Ah."

"Exactly. And now I must undo it. Be a wallflower and dried-up, desperate spinster and all that." She glanced at Priya. "Please tell me it was worth it?"

Priya smiled slowly "We will make sure of it."

AMANDINE'S IDEA OF a restrained birthday celebration involved a fountain of champagne pouring from the pitcher in the hand of a marble statue of a nymph. There were flowers, music, and circulating delicacies on gold platters. There was dancing, because Lady Wentworth could not abide an evening without dancing.

And, of course, there were fireworks to rival royal celebrations, from Versailles to St. James's Palace.

Londoners gathered in the streets on the earl's birthday because everyone knew the fireworks would be visible all the way to the river.

There was every luxury, every entertainment, every extravagance.

There were marquesses and dukes and a princess.

But no Keir.

By the time the fireworks were ready, Sybil had taken several turns around the house, and still no Keir. Sophie was in attendance with an elderly chaperone, despite the fact that she had not yet had her coming out. It was no great surprise Keir had not accompanied her—he only seldom crossed the threshold of the Taunton residence, especially if Sybil was at home. Anything to be sure no one linked their names together. He was careful, honest, rule-bound.

Lonely.

She knew it, even if he did not. She tasted it in every kiss, saw it in every glance.

She ought to be a great deal more furious about it, but mostly she was confused. He kept everyone at bay by choice. The day his mother died giving birth to Sophie was the day he had changed. He went from a lad who climbed trees with her to a young man who schooled his every expression and spoke very little. Even she had not been able to needle anything out of him, and she was very, very good at needling him.

But she was not *Lady* Sybil, merely *Miss* Taunton.

And he was the heir to a marquess, even if he had none of the usual lesser honorary titles because his father would not give them up.

But some things had not changed.

Sybil was not going to wait around for him. He needed to be dragged out of his cave once in a while.

And she needed *him*.

She did not *want* to need him, but she had learned long ago that that had very little bearing on the matter.

Sybil slipped from the crowded house, skirting the men congregating in the back garden, shouting to each other about gunpowder and distance. She knew every inch of pathway and the brittle lawn spiked with hoarfrost. The crack in the wall at the very back, behind the plum tree, had never been repaired. In fact, it had widened considerably during the years she and Keir used it as a thoroughfare.

She climbed through it, knowing to duck so that she did not bash her head on the oak tree on the other side. Montgomery House was dark save a candle burning in an upstairs window. The household staff were gathered in the mews between the houses, waiting for the fireworks. They did not see Sybil as she crossed the formal garden's white gravel paths. She felt Keir standing at the glass door, watching her, before she even saw him. It was always like that. That had never changed, even when everything else had.

He stepped back when she opened the door, neither of them saying a word.

He held her gaze for a long, long moment.

Then he exhaled roughly and reached for her, hauling her up against him, his mouth closing over hers. She was already kissing him back. The hunger they hid from the world, even from each other, would not be ignored for long. It was madness.

And it was glorious.

The kiss was urgent, desperate. All consuming. Heat washed through her, expectant, eager. Impatient. He walked her backward through the parlor, still kissing her, still tasting her, right into a small music room no one ever used. He lifted her onto a table, stepping between her knees in a decisive move that made her moan. His hardness pressed against her, sending sparks into her belly.

There were still no words, none needed, none wanted. Only hands and teeth and mouth sucking at the tender skin behind her ear. He dragged his hands up her legs, widening her thighs, fingertips moving over her stockings to her bare skin, up, up, until he finally, finally reached her heated center, wet and swollen just at the thought of him.

He parted her lips, gliding thick fingers over her bud once, twice, and then plunging into her heat. She gasped, writhing against him. He always knew just how to touch her, just how to wring every ounce of pleasure from her body in the brief, furtive moments they allowed themselves. She rubbed her palm over the swell of his cock, gripping it through his breeches.

But he did not stop, not for a second, not even when he groaned into her neck. His fingers kept at their work, stroking her, curling inside to reach that sensitive spot that made her eyes close and her breath stutter. Again and again until her thighs quivered, until the pleasure coiled and tightened and then released, wave after wave of sensation.

She was still panting, her pulse racing as she helped free him from the confines of his breeches. He was hard and swollen for her, the tip of his cock glistening. She curled her hand around him, pumping as she drew him nearer, until she could drag it through her slick folds. His eyes darkened. She urged him closer, demanded it.

He slid through her wetness, the stretch of her body accommodating her stinging in a delicious way. His breath was harsh and rough in her ear. He splayed his big hand over her spine and took her weight while angling her so she could take more of him. Her head fell back, and she gasped at every thrust. She was so full, so anchored to him. She wanted more—she always wanted more.

He plunged deeper, slower, every stroke deliberate. Another climax began to build as she answered thrust for thrust, moan for moan. When it streaked up her thighs, she thought she was seeing exploding colors, but it was only the fireworks through the glass. They were bathed in flashing, jewel-toned lights as Keir gritted his teeth, refusing to alter his pace until she came again, and then he pulled free and released into the handkerchief he had clawed from his pocket.

They shuddered against each other, foreheads pressed close, eyes shut.

All without a single word passing between them.

As usual.

Chapter Six

Just because she was a spinster long on the shelf and about to embarrass herself at the Willoughby ball did not mean that Sybil had to look the part. So if she washed her hair three more times than was necessary to scrub away the last of the tea-stain hue, that was perfectly within her rights.

And if she wondered if Keir would notice, it was no one else's business.

Also, utterly ridiculous.

Because it was not *her* business either.

He was not her business.

He was not the boy who had met her at the gap in the garden wall to share sweets and secrets and a laugh, that surprised, rusty laugh of his, which only too seldom made an appearance. He was not the boy who had broken another boy's nose for calling Sybil a guttersnipe. Or the boy who had taught her a secret language using the light of a lantern, such as smugglers were said to use in Cornwall.

He was not a boy at all, of course. He was a man grown, more solemn and serious with each and every day.

Except for those brief moments that took them both over. A collision, a conflagration. It made her miss him all the more. Made her crave him with every fiber of her being. The girl from the gutter and the marquess.

It did not matter. The girl from the gutter was a little busy at present.

She did not have time to replay the way he had groaned into her neck, the play of the blue light from the fireworks on his cheekbones. The way her body came alive for him, each and every time.

Willoughby House was lit from top window to kitchen cellar, golden light spilling over the bare rosebushes, the slender trees shining like swords in the cold mist. The heavy London fog settled low, thick and smoky, as coal fires were lit against the unseasonable chill. The wheels of carriages echoed behind her as Sybil made her way between the lit torches.

She stepped inside and handed her cloak to a footman but ducked down the hall, away from the ballroom and the master of ceremonies waiting to announce the guests. The house simply sparkled: the polished marble floors under her dancing slippers (her toes were already cold), the crystal beads of the chandeliers overhead, the ornate gilt frames showing off paintings of generations of family spaniels. And one cow roughly the size of a barn. Hothouse lilies stood sentry, perfuming the air so thickly that she coughed a little as she made her way to the ladies' retiring room.

It was too early in the evening for the ladies to crowd inside for a rest between dancing sets, or to fix a dropped hem. Sybil ducked behind the painted screens used to give some privacy to the row of chamber pots. There were baskets of cloths, perfume, a washstand with jasmine-scented soap.

Sybil unrolled the notices she had tucked inside her reticule. This was not her usual work for the society, but as she was here anyway, she may as well make herself useful. Her friend Clara used to do this before she married a retired captain and moved to the seaside. They had many secret members, who would never be associated with the society and therefore could work covertly for these sorts of things.

Sybil was not such a member.

At least not in London. Not in Mayfair. Not anymore.

She pinned the papers to the fabric at the back of the folding screen: the names of men who ought to be avoided for a woman's own safety, and proof of their transgressions. Fortune hunters who pretended they were well-to-do. Widowers whose wives had died under mysterious circumstances. How to procure certain teas and tinctures. Midwives who did not judge or ask too many questions. A hastily scrawled drawing of how to use a hatpin to do as much damage with as little force as necessary.

More information than the Bow Street Runners could gather. Sybil felt more than a bit smug about that, actually.

She was still smirking when she slipped into the ballroom.

And nearly collided with Lady Pontefract.

And her daughter.

Sybil was going to have to eat crow with a serving of humble pie for dessert.

Lovely.

"You!" Lady Pontefract all but screeched. Her brown ringlets bobbed with outrage. Guests glanced in their direction, eager for more gossip.

Sybil kept her smile in place. "Lady Pontefract, I understand that you are upset."

"Upset?"

"Maman, please," Lady Violetta said. She was tall and slender and beautiful. Her smile was genuine, soft. A little bit desperate. She did not appear to care for the attention.

"I assure you this is all a misunderstanding," Sybil continued soothingly. "Which I will make clear with all alacrity, I promise you. In the meantime, it can only help that we are seen to be friendly and unaffected, don't you think?"

Lady Pontefract paused.

"It will prove the rumors false better than anything I could ever say or do, and your daughter will come away with everyone noting her graciousness and dignity." And Sybil's indignity, but it would not be the first time. She enjoyed her escapades and did not regret them, but it would be foolish to pretend there was not a price to pay every time.

Lady Pontefract released her breath, gathered for another screech. Her expression turned abruptly mild and bland. It was slightly terrifying. She might have made a good Spinster. "I take your point, Miss Taunton."

"Thank you, Maman," her daughter murmured.

"And how do you intend to rectify this situation?" Lady Pontefract snapped from behind her fan. It dripped with pink and pearl tassels. If she grew any more agitated with the fluttering of it, her eyes would be in very great danger.

Before Sybil could reply, Keir appeared behind her.

She knew he was there before he said a word. The attention of the other guests was a honed arrow, nocked at the bowstring and aimed directly at them. No escaping.

Keir Montgomery did not blend into the wallpaper at the best of times. He was too large, too rugged, even with the fine cut of his coat, the engraved gold buttons. The hewn line of his jaw, the patient, piercing green of his eyes.

It would have been so much easier if he stank of herring and old cheese.

He smelled like rain and wood smoke.

Unforgivable.

The absolute blighter.

"Lady Pontefract." He bowed politely. His expression warmed. "Lady Violetta." And then turned inscrutable. "Miss Taunton."

"Lord Blackburn," Sybil murmured to him when no other chatter was forthcoming. The gossips would be in their glory if the four of them stood about awkwardly staring at each other in silence. Not to mention that Lady Pontefract was about to explode, which would not do anyone any favors. "You should dance."

"Oh, should I?" he replied, faintly amused. Violetta blinked at him as if surprised. Sybil did not blame her. His brief smile, rarely seen, was devastating.

"Yes. Dance with Lady Violetta, and I will stand with the other wallflowers and look appropriately subdued."

"Is that a skill you have?" He sounded dubious.

"I have many skills." *She* sounded positively suggestive, and she had not meant to. His eyes flared. Heat bloomed in her lower belly in response. That would not do. Not here. "Just go so I can fix this as I promised."

"What if I want to dance with *you?*" he asked so softly that only she could hear him, and she was not convinced she had heard him correctly.

"You don't," she pointed out. Was he flirting? The man did not flirt. With anyone. And certainly not with her. This was against all of the rules.

"I don't?" he said. "You sound very sure."

Was this his idea of revenge? She had thought him too proper for that.

"I am sure." She did not know what this game was, but she had no intention of playing. She did not play games where she lost before she even started. It was hardly sporting. And the possibility for devastation was too great.

"Did you hit your head on the way here?" she asked, crossly.

He chuckled.

Out loud.

In the middle of a crowded ballroom.

Both Sybil and Violetta turned slowly to stare at him.

"Lady Violetta," Keir said, his voice whisky and cream. Delicious. "It appears that we have our marching orders." He held out his hand. "Will you dance?"

Violetta smiled prettily. "Of course, my lord."

They were perfect together. Polished, gracious. Refined in a way that drew the eye, held it.

When Sybil went to move away, Lady Pontefract's hand closed over her arm. Her nails were sharp. "A moment, Miss Taunton?"

Sybil stifled a sigh. She had been so close to escape. She could already feel the pitying glances, but they were nothing. She was used to them. "Yes, Lady Pontefract?"

"I do wonder how that rumor began in the first place?"

"As I said, a misunderstanding." It wasn't, of course. She had known exactly what she was doing and had done it anyway. Although, in all fairness, she had not seen Keir in weeks, not anywhere except from her front step. She did not know what he did with his days. She had heard he was courting, but one heard all manner of things.

Such as that Sybil had stolen a duke's favorite coat, embroidered in Italy, the one he would not stop boasting about, and had put it on a donkey.

Not a perfect example, perhaps, as it was true.

And the duke deserved it. She felt no remorse over it whatsoever. The donkey had been well compensated with ear scratches and apples. She *would* feel remorse, however, if she had truly interfered with Violetta's prospects. Or with Keir's. It had certainly not been her intention, despite everything.

Lady Pontefract knew none of this, of course. She only knew that a wild hoyden of questionable breeding had trampled through her carefully orchestrated plans for her daughter. Keir was the catch of the Season, every Season. He was a marquess. He was handsome and courteous. His brows had that little divot between them when he was studying Sybil as though she were a runaway animal from the Royal Menagerie. He was strong enough to hold her up against a garden wall.

"Do not obstruct my daughter," Lady Pontefract said.

Sybil did not stifle her sigh this time. Sometimes it was best to get to the meat of it straightaway. "Lady Pontefract, let's be frank, shall we? It will save us both a lot of fuss and bother."

"Do go on."

"Do you really believe that any marquess, least of all Lord Blackburn, bound to duty as he is, would throw your daughter over for someone like me?"

Lady Pontefract narrowed her eyes as though it was a riddle. Her expression cleared as the music swelled and Keir swung Violetta into a waltz. They belonged in a painting. The gold light caressed her hair, her delicate nose. The white of her gown glowed. And he looked like some warrior of old, strong, confident. They were made for this world and it was made for them.

"You are quite correct, Miss Taunton," Lady Pontefract finally said.

One point, Sybil.

It did not feel like winning. It felt more like a splinter, disagreeable and hard to ignore.

Sybil went to stand by the row of chairs set out for wallflowers and chaperones to do her penance, though it was hardly required. Not with Violetta glowing like an angel. Sybil's gown was pretty and fashionable, in a stunning shade of green, but she did not glow. Her reticule was stretched out of shape from smuggling in posters that accused half the men in this room. She remembered the damp smell of the rookeries: stone and coal smoke and mud. Wet garbage. Urine.

She did not remember her first parents very well, only brief memories of the smell of her mother's medicine and her father's clumsy hands trying to braid her wispy hair the rare times he was back from being at sea.

A little disdain from the *ton* was nothing.

And it was not *exactly* disdain. Only an unspoken agreement that she was tolerated here, sometimes even fondly, but she did not truly belong. Not when there were men like Keir to be married off and young debutantes like Violetta, angelic in their beauty and flawless in their ancestral ties. Her grandfather had been a duke, her great-grandmother the third daughter of a prince.

But if there was even a hint that the natural order of things might be threatened, the *ton* reacted immediately. Peppering the air with comments meant to sting, like little wasps. Reminders.

Lines drawn in the sand.

Luckily, they were not very creative. She had heard them all before. She did not even bother to fight a yawn when it slipped through.

Better than the barest flinch when Miss Renfield stopped deliberately within earshot. "How desperate," she said. "As if a marquess would marry someone like *her*."

"What can you expect? Blood will out."

Sybil considered turning around with suggestions for better insults. More interesting barbs. Something *entertaining*. She did not. She would have, had she not been proving a point about her connections to the Marquess Blackburn. They were *meant* to think such things about her tonight. Her unsuitability.

And they did not even know about the time she had stolen a letter from an earl during a ball and slid down the banister, chased by two footmen. Or when she had jumped into the Serpentine in order to draw attention away from a debutante avoiding a duke's son.

They did not know her at all, truly.

It helped. A little.

So did the perpetually cheerful Lord Victor Bailey, second son of an earl and still too good for her, but it did not matter, as their only interest in each other was saving one another from boredom. He was a hero, in his own way.

"Dance with me, Miss Taunton," Victor said, too loudly as always. His golden curls flopped over his forehead in a way that made many girls sigh. Sybil only itched to push it back where it belonged and slap some pomade through it. "No one is nearly as fun as you are, and they all come with sticky matrimonial strings and expectations."

He did not intend to be rude and would have been shocked at the accusation. Sybil, though not a wallflower in the strictest sense, *was* a spinster. She could not be expected to marry particularly well, at least in this particular crowd, and so no one much worried about dancing twice in a row or being seen alone chatting on the balcony. She was not on the market.

The market did not care for her.

She did not much care for the market either, to be fair.

The sight of Keir's legs in his kilt would not change that.

And anyway, Victor's cheerful candor was refreshing. It had nothing to do with her and everything to do with the rules. There was many a fortune hunter who would have disregarded those rules for a crack at her dowry. Which was exactly why her parents let it be known that she did not have one.

It was not true. Her dowry and inheritance were substantial, but to protect her from fortune hunters and families who would not respect her or treat her well, they had chosen to hide it from Society.

Victor danced with more enthusiasm than finesse. Sybil laughed as he whirled her too fast and too wildly until they were both dizzy. They danced another set while Keir escorted Violetta to the refreshment tables and procured her a glass of ratafia, frowning at Sybil's display. As ratafia was created by the devil himself, Sybil much preferred to keep dancing. She danced until her feet ached and her hair slipped its elegant twist, until her breath burned and she stopped seeing Keir's hand clasped around Violetta's waist.

"I heard a story about you today," Victor said, thrusting a glass of champagne into her hand.

"I am quite sure you did," Sybil replied drily. "I assure you, Lord Blackburn is not courting me."

"Obviously." Victor dismissed it immediately.

Hmph.

Valid. But *hmph* nonetheless.

"No, this is about Fortingham's."

"I was only there because the weather was dreadful," Sybil said, forcing her tone to be light. Positively effervescent. "And then I could not help myself—I had to poke a little fun at the marquess. He is so proper. Was it terribly wicked of me, do you think?"

Victor laughed. "Blackburn deserved it, I'm sure. The man is dour."

Sybil found she did not like that. It was suddenly very tempting to shove Victor's head into the punch bowl.

Very tempting.

"No, it's only that the betting book went missing last night." He looked around furtively. "I should not say so out loud. It's a secret. The club is terribly embarrassed."

Ha! Good.

Sybil blinked. "Lord Bailey, are you asking me if I stole a… What was it? A book from the club? I did not think you read in such places."

He studied her, then laughed again. "I suppose not. I fancied myself a hero returning with the booty, like the eagle standard of the Roman army."

Sybil's expression remained impassive. A touch bewildered.

"Never mind, Miss Taunton," Victor added. "I am being a fool. Shall we dance more? I can almost feel my lungs again."

Sybil smiled back. "Let's."

"What a shame you don't have a dowry," he sighed.

IF ONE MORE person smiled at him in commiseration and suggested Sybil was a desperate wallflower no better than she should be, Keir would hold their head inside the punch bowl.

Even if it was a dowager who smelled like liniment.

Not to mention that he'd woken up to the rumor that he had three mistresses. By later afternoon, it was said he was caught frolicking with *four* different courtesans outside a brothel.

Keir did not have a mistress, never mind four courtesans. And he did not frolic.

Certainly not outside in winter.

He wasn't an idiot.

Except that he was. Clearly.

Because only an idiot mooned after a feral madwoman while courting another woman. Who had the perfect bloodlines, the perfect estate bordering his, the perfect dowry. The perfect smile.

Sybil's smile was not perfect.

It was not Lady Violetta's fault that she had been handpicked by his father. Only months dead and the old despot was still trying to control him from the grave. He couldn't even swan about in heaven—or more likely, hell. He had to meddle and control.

Lady Violetta was lovely.

And Keir was an idiot.

Simple as that.

He could not picture her walking the Highland crags, the wind catching at her bonnet strings. Walking in the rain.

Climbing a trellis into her own bedroom.

He could not picture her letting down her hair, stepping out of her chemise. Climbing into his lap. Naked.

All things he could picture Sybil doing. Had *seen* her doing. Had helped her to do.

The way she had curled up in his lap, the firelight playing over her hair, her soft cheek. The smell of warm skin and soap and rain. How he had to hold her at an angle so she would notice his erection pressing against the placket of his breeches, desperate at her nearness. They both knew where that led. But he wanted that quiet moment, so rare between them.

It was torture.

Perfect, beautiful torture.

That carefully constructed wall between them was crumbling as though it were made of sugar paste.

He was known for his sense of duty and responsibility, but there was absolutely nothing dutiful about the way he felt around Sybil. *Uncivilized* was more accurate. Starving.

Savage.

His monster of a father would have blamed it on his mother's Scottish blood. On Keir's own selfish weakness. A hundred things. But the only culprit was right now laughing as Lord Bailey whirled her too fast between several disapproving couples. If she had been an earl's legitimate daughter, they would have smiled, murmured about her *joie de vivre*. But Sybil was different.

In all the best ways.

He always knew where she was in a room. It was like that from the first moment he saw her: a glimpse through the crack in the garden wall. An unexpected voice, a silly jest to make him laugh when he was struggling not to give in to the pain of the new bruises on his cheek. She had proceeded to scamper up the plum tree and drop down into the grass behind him, dress hem muddy, hair in a braid ornamented with twigs and more than a few leaves. Her immediate offer to sneak into the very elegant Montgomery townhouse and put frogs in his father's bed. When he pointed out his father was a marquess, she only shrugged and said, "Worms, then."

For years they met at the garden wall, leaving notes, posies of flowers, sugared almonds.

And then his father noticed the orphan girl next door.

And everything changed.

Keir had spent considerable energy pretending not to notice her, not to see her after that.

But he always, *always* saw her.

His father had never been allowed to know that. Not one glance, not for one moment. Even as a young lad, Keir knew that in his bones. His father already sneered at the Tauntons adopting a half-starved orphan girl covered in mud from some alley and making her their daughter. He had refused to allow her inside the Montgomery house and sneered when she made too much noise in the Tauntons' own back garden, which was often.

Keir did not make noise. He did not draw attention.

Except to keep his father's attention away from Sybil.

He went to Eton, to Oxford, to Parliament. He did what was expected of him. He pretended so well that everyone thought of him only as a dutiful heir, a marquess devoted to responsibility. Assumed that he worshipped at the altar of the family name, like his father. Forgot that his mother was Scottish, that *he* was

Scottish enough not to want to sacrifice every ounce of joy to a British title.

Too late.

But his father was right about one thing and one thing only: Keir had an estate to take care of. Tenants and farmers and villagers. A little sister who rolled her eyes at him every time he said anything at all. Who put porridge in her headmistress's shoes.

Honestly, he was damned proud of that last one. He had already spoken to the headmistress, who had promptly decided she would much rather take up some other post that had nothing to do with schools or young ladies. Their father would have sent Sophie right back, demanded she apologize in some humiliating way, and paid for a new wing of the school.

Their father had been a rigid, dictatorial, cruel ass.

Keir wanted to be anything but that.

Even as his father's voice barked in his head.

He bowed over Lady Violetta's hand, trying not to feel like an ogre with a fairy princess. "Another dance, Lady Violetta?"

"It would be an honor, Lord Blackburn."

Honor.

How he hated the word.

CHAPTER SEVEN

S YBIL SLIPPED OUT as soon as Victor was distracted by the arrival of a young debutante with a dowry of six thousand pounds. Just as well. Because *she* was distracted by Keir. Again. As usual.

Unacceptable.

He could take his rumbly voice and his strong jaw and his muscular arms and jump headfirst into the Thames.

She had done her duty. She had accepted the disdain of the guests, the affable pity, the shaking of heads over her wild ways, clearly a result of her birth despite the Wentworths' careful upbringing. Violetta was the apple of Keir's eye once more. Everything was as it should be. The proper order of the universe was restored, hurrah.

Sybil could go home and eat an entire cake now, if she wanted.

She deserved cake. Mostly because she firmly believed that every spinster and wallflower deserved cake. And wine.

Access to her own inheritance. The ability to own property. Vengeance.

But tonight, cake would have to do.

She accepted her cloak from a footman, but before she could finally escape the stuffy, crowded house, Lord Willoughby's annoyed voice carried down the hall. "I won't have those damned posters in my house."

As the purveyor of *those damned posters*, Sybil stepped back into the shadows and waited. No need to draw his notice. Although the harried housemaid running to keep up with him would no doubt have welcomed the interruption.

"Throw those in the fire," Lord Willoughby barked.

"Whatever is the matter?" Lady Willoughby glided in, her smile very pointed. "Your voice does carry, my lord."

"Those damned posters from those *women*. In my house!"

Lady Willoughby's smile did not waver. "Oh, is that all?"

"I want them tossed."

"Of course, dear."

He stalked away, snatching a glass of wine from a footman's tray. Lady Willoughby sent the housemaid a grim look. "Put those back where you found them."

"Yes, your ladyship."

Grinning, Sybil made a note to mention it to Priya. A sore ego and an ally in the Willoughby house. Either could prove useful.

Outside, the night air was cold enough to mist her breath and glitter over the windows of the hundred carriages lined up along the street, waiting for the ball to wind down. It was not likely to for several more hours. Horses stamped their feet. She had sent her own carriage home as soon as she arrived. She much preferred to continue on foot all the way to Spinster House, despite the damage it might do to her reputation. She failed to see how being outside was so egregious.

Until the rain started.

It turned the streets to silver and her pretty silk slippers to paper. She huddled into her cloak and waved at a hackney coachman. There were always a few driving around the square, waiting for several parties to let out. He nodded to her, and she stepped out to wait for him.

A carriage suddenly pulled out, barreling toward her, coming out of the queue. She heard the creak of wheels going too fast, the crack of hooves. She stumbled back, the wind of it on her face, the flash of the carriage window so close to her nose that it nearly left a mark.

And a great splash of half-frozen mud splattering all over her. Thoroughly.

"Perfect," Sybil muttered, wiping mud from her cheek and flinging it to the ground. Her heart hammered in her throat. "Just perfect."

The carriage did not stop; the driver did not even glance back. She sucked in a cold breath.

"Are you all right, miss?" Three nearby coachmen scrambled off their seats, gathering around her, eyes wide.

She did not have time to answer before they were jostled aside and Keir was suddenly there, big, warm hands closing over her shoulders. His cool, impassive expression was lost behind a fearsome scowl. He looked wild, enraged. His hands were gentle. "*Sybil!*"

She blinked at him. "What are you doing here?"

"What are *you* doing here?" Rain soaked into his thick hair. "You could have been killed."

The coachmen nodded behind him in unison like a Greek chorus.

"I'm fine," Sybil assured them with a smile. She wiped more mud from her ear. How had it managed to get inside her *ear*?

Keir stared at her with disconcerting intensity, as if he could see down to her bones. He was thorough, inspecting her for bruises.

"I'm fine," she said again, softer.

The coachmen were just as scandalized as Keir. She forgot to mention that she put herself in much worse situations on a regular basis. A traffic mishap was an ordinary danger on a London street.

"That almost never happens! Must be three sheets to the wind, that one."

"That bastard didn't even stop."

"Swear he sped up!"

"Did you see whose carriage that was?" Keir demanded of them. "I want a name."

"No family crest, nothing. Couldn't even see his face, all wrapped up in that scarf."

Sybil's smile died.

No identifying crest, a scarf worn high, a hat worn low.

She knew what that meant.

It was no accident.

She clawed her smile back. No need to worry the coachmen, who were staring at her with wide, frazzled eyes. The one on the left might start weeping.

"Where's your carriage?" Keir asked.

"I don't have one. I'm not going far."

He stared at her for a long moment as if she had suggested she liked to leap off the spire of St. Paul's Cathedral on a regular basis just to see if she could fly.

She *had* climbed out of a cathedral window once, but he did not need to know that.

Not if the muscle twitching in his jaw was any indication. "My carriage is just here. Get in."

His carriage was all perfectly polished mahogany, with gleaming gold accents, swaying lanterns at each corner. It was understated and practical while also being the height of luxury. Exactly right for the Marquess Blackburn. It would be warm and pleasant inside.

"Really, I'm not going far," Sybil said instead.

"Sybil."

"It will not help the rumors I've just worked so hard to squash."

"*Sybil.*" That calm tone, patient, knowing, faintly exasperated. A hint of the Keir she used to know. Missed desperately, even now. "I am not letting you go home alone covered in mud, in rain that is rapidly turning to snow after nearly being run over." His voice dropped. "You're cold."

She did shiver, though it had nothing to do with the temperature. "I am certain you need to see Lady Violetta home."

He frowned. "Her mother just left with a headache. How did you know?"

"A lucky guess." She knew Lady Pontefract. And the marriage-minded mamas of the *ton*. And her own luck.

"I can take you both home," he decided. "The carriage can easily seat four. I am sure she won't mind."

Sybil knew that some battles needed to be lost for the war to be won. And that sometimes a frontal attack was not the best tactic. She nodded mutely and let him help her into his carriage. It was just as warm as she had expected, with hot bricks for the feet, plump cushions, dark blue velvet curtains.

And if he thought she would stay there, he was mad.

Her choices were thus: being trapped in this perfect carriage with perfect Keir and his perfect fiancée while covered in mud to make perfectly polite conversation. *Or* run on foot back home in the freezing drizzle and hope no one else tried to mow her down.

No contest.

She flung herself out of the carriage the moment Keir strode away, waving a farewell at the coachman who called after her, alarmed, and then she proceeded to sprint down the pavement in a way no gently bred lady would have ever contemplated.

And it felt good.

FINDING HIS CARRIAGE empty did *not* feel good.

Keir's hands curled into fists and the muscles at the back of his neck seized abruptly. The rain was turning to ice, but it was probably steaming as it hit his shoulders. He helped Lady Violetta inside, keeping his stoic, polite mask secure. He glared up at his coachman, Arthur, who was already holding up his hands placatingly, and with more than a hint of alarm. Keir smoothed out his scowl. Marquesses did not scowl. Marquesses did not go chasing after wayward ladies in the middle of the night. They did not chase ladies at all.

To hell with that.

"Where is she?" he demanded.

"She ran off as soon as you were out of earshot, my lord," Arthur replied. "Clever girl."

The streets weren't safe. They were cold and dark and slippery and filled with coachmen who were not careful. But she *was* clever and, moreover, would not appreciate his worry. He had no right to it. It was all out of balance. The hiss of panic through his chest was overblown. Unnecessary. Real all the same.

He nodded and climbed in to sit across from Violetta. He would see her home and then make sure that Sybil was also at home. Safe. Warm.

"Your friend was very kind," Violetta said softly as the horses were urged into a steady walk.

"My friend?" He tried not to sound as impatient as he felt. Why was it taking so long? Anything could happen to Sybil. To a woman who was recently locked in the cellar of a man he very much wanted to strangle. He had made inquiries, in point of fact. But the Marquess of Eastbourne was in the process of being stripped of his title and had already fled to the Continent. Keir had toyed with the idea of finding him. And by toyed, he meant he had made plans, talked to the people he would need, both legal and criminal, but had not yet committed to action.

Not yet did not mean *never*.

In the meantime, he did have men stationed at the docks, waiting to alert him if Eastbourne dared return to England.

He also had a beautiful woman sitting across from him waiting for him to respond like a gentleman instead of whatever it was he was doing. "I beg your pardon?"

"Miss Taunton," Violetta elaborated, and Keir wondered if he had thought about Sybil so hard that he had conjured a conversation about her. With the lady he was meant to be courting. *Bloody hell.* "She put herself in my mother's path, which took no small amount of courage."

Keir nodded. "She was sorry to have caused you trouble or

embarrassment."

"Yes, I believe she was."

There was not much to say after that. Remarks on the evening's entertainment, the celebrated violinist hired to play throughout the supper, the flowers. The turn in the weather, if the Thames might ice over to allow for skating.

All very appropriate.

Sybil would have said half a dozen wild and unsuitable things by now.

He should not find that so charming.

The carriage finally pulled up to the Pontefract townhouse, where the curtains in an upstairs window jerked closed. Violetta smiled. "My mother."

"Ah."

Keir stepped down and offered his arm. Violetta alighted like a winter sprite, her thick white cloak edged with fur, diamonds glittering in the frigid air. Keir waited for the butler to open the door before bowing, as was expected. "Lady Violetta, I bid you goodnight."

And then, as soon as the door closed again, Keir thundered back to his carriage. "Home, Arthur."

As he was not a stupid man, Arthur did not linger.

SYBIL MADE IT to Spinster House in record time. There was ice in her hair, quite possibly in her ears too, and her feet were soaked through in her pathetic excuse for dancing slippers. But she was smiling. Invigorated.

Not at all wondering if Keir was even now seeing Lady Violetta home.

Or kissing the back of her hand.

He would never—that was too forward.

But so was cradling Sybil on his lap. Taking her against the garden wall. Gripping her bare thighs.

But Sybil was Sybil. She already knew the rules were different.

She tossed her sodden cloak on a hook and determined not to waste the rest of her evening thinking about Keir Montgomery, who would definitely not be thinking of her. He would be reading something serious, drinking scotch. Looking over the terms of Violetta's dowry.

Gah.

Sybil went straight to the kitchen for a very large piece of cake and took it to the ballroom and the basket of knives and the incongruous hay bale set up in one corner, on which Matilda had painted the face of a gentleman who had once insulted her. The mustache was a thing of legend.

They liked to aim for it.

Peony was already there, dangling from a rope attached to the ceiling.

Home. There was nothing quite like it.

Keir gave serious consideration to climbing Sybil's trellis again, which was when he started questioning his own sanity.

He was overreacting.

It was not Sybil's fault that he found he could not breathe if he did not know she was safe. He had seen that carriage barrel past her, had watched the force of the wind set her back on her heels. She could have been trampled. Tossed to the ground. Broken in a dozen different ways. Locked in a damned cellar.

But she wasn't.

And he still could not stop it from repeating in his mind like a terrible play with an unwilling audience of one.

There was no light in her window. She could already be under the blankets.

A much nicer image to play in his mind's eye as he went to sit in his chair and brood at the view from his window. First, he would make certain she was safe even if it was forward of him. And presumptuous. She did not have to know about it.

Which might have worked a charm if he had not instantly scrawled her name at the top of the paper on his desk.

Sybil was dangling from the ceiling when the note arrived.

It had been delivered to her house, and from there a footman had sent it here. Her hands were cramped around the rope as she turned in a lazy circle, peering down. "A note for me?"

"Yes, miss," Peter replied, unfazed by the ladies dangling from the ceiling.

"At this hour?" Peony asked. "That does not bode well."

"Perhaps not," Sybil admitted. When notes arrived at Spinster House in the middle of the night, they did not generally herald an invitation to take tea. There was more often than not subterfuge involved. Criminal activity.

Not a message written by a marquess.

"A love letter?" Peony asked, grimacing. Peony did not care for love letters. She did not understand the fuss.

"Not exactly."

Where the bloody hell was she?

Why had she not replied? Was she in trouble?

A footman left her house, but he did not come to knock at Keir's door. He walked away down the street. She was not safely at home.

Keir would have followed him, if his little sister had not chosen that very moment to take ten years off his life.

Sybil,

When you are nearly flattened by a carriage and then offered an escort home, you do not run away on foot without a word. In inclement weather. In the middle of the night. Pray, send word that you are unharmed. I am not playing at games. Blackburn.

Sybil read the note three times, which was two times too many. There was no reason to read it more than once. It was hardly poetry. There was nothing private or personal about it.

Though he *did* seem worried for her wellbeing.

Which was kind.

Or merely dutiful?

This was the *Most* Stoic and Most Dutiful Marquess Blackburn, after all.

"Keir, why are you sitting in the dark like a bloody specter," Sophie yelped—once she had stopped screaming. His ears echoed with it.

"Why are *you* lurking about the house so late?" he returned. "And don't say 'bloody.'"

She rolled her eyes. "I couldn't sleep." With her hair knotted in rags and her slippers peeking out from a thick nightdress, she looked like his little sister again, not just the girl ready to be a debutante who rolled her eyes every time he said anything. "What are *you* doing?"

"Also not sleeping."

"I came to borrow a book," she said, then sighed. "But everything in this house is so deadly dull. Farming techniques and the history of water clocks and those etiquette manuals Father loved so much."

"You clearly have not read those manuals—how would you know if they are dull?"

She rolled her eyes again. One day he would keep a tally of how many times she did that in one conversation. "I would rather start a proper bonfire with them."

He did not blame her. If she only knew how many times he had been forced to read them, as well as every dry treatise dating back to the Romans. Dissertations on the Empire. Lectures. Papers. Broken rulers over his knuckles when he got something wrong. When he dared say at eight years old that he would much rather climb trees or learn to play the pianoforte than learn Latin.

"Even finishing schools have the odd novel," she muttered.

He hadn't thought about the library in the house. Everything was mostly the same as it had always been. Almost as though he were secretly afraid his father would come barreling out of his study shouting if Keir changed a single candlestick. But it was not his study any longer. It was Keir's.

"I'm not going back to that school," Sophie said defiantly.

"I know. They won't have you," Keir pointed out drily. "I've already made other arrangements."

She frowned briefly before tugging her shawl closer together. "I should have guessed you would want to be rid of me as quickly as possible."

"That's not it," he said, honestly surprised. "Girls go to finishing schools." Didn't they?

"Never mind."

Dear Most Stoic and Dutiful Lord Blackburn,

I am perfectly capable of looking after myself. I am, however, sorry if you were worried. I can't think why. I am a very staid and dull person and never cause trouble.

Dear Sybil,

Ha.

Dear Marquess of All Things Proper,

Is that any way to speak to a lady? I am sure I am offended.

S

Hoyden,

If I believed you, I am sure I would be most apologetic.

K

Sybil grinned. She couldn't help it.

"Stay focused," Peony grumbled when her dagger missed the target's mustache by many inches.

"I *am* focused."

"Only on those scraps of paper. Who are they from?" Peony glanced at the first note, with its precisely signed name, and groaned. "I should have known. That look on your face."

"What about it?"

"It's how Matilda and Emmeline look at each other. And how Clara used to look at Captain Thorn before they got married." She shook her head, disgusted. "Sybil, really. I expected better of you."

"Don't be ridiculous."

She wasn't for marrying.

And Keir wasn't for her.

CHAPTER EIGHT

T HE NEXT MORNING, Sybil joined the others for breakfast, where only half of a plum cake was set out among the sweet rolls and the toasted bread and coddled eggs. She did not feel the least bit guilty. Some nights called for cake. Even when she noticed the little note left by Mrs. Werthers, the cook. It read: *Sybil Taunton, clean up your crumbs next time.*

Priya drank tea while Peony spooned a truly indecent amount of raspberry preserves onto her bread. Her hair was damp. She always started the day with a swim, just as she ended it. Emmeline drank cup after cup of coffee with no food at all. Matilda mostly ate cheese. Sybil helped herself to eggs and roasted potatoes and a baked apple.

"Mrs. Werthers said you ate half a cake last night," Priya said.

"Yes, and it was delicious," Sybil replied.

"You only eat that much cake when there is a problem."

"Not a problem. Only that someone tried to run me over with a carriage outside the Willoughby ball." And Keir's notes had reminded her too much of what used to be. "I decided I deserved cake."

The others blinked at her. Matilda scowled. "So you did. That's rather rude."

"I thought so too. But I do not even have a turned ankle to show for it. A Spinster is made of sterner stuff than that." She pushed a piece of chive around on her plate. "It could have been an accident. It *probably* was."

"Did it feel like one?" Priya asked.

"I'm not sure," Sybil admitted. "If it wasn't, I assume it would be because of the betting book? A warning off from some lord with his wig all askew?" *This* was why Priya set the assignments and not the others. Sybil ought to have remembered that. Priya was careful. Methodical. Sybil was not. What had Keir called her once, when he climbed a tree to rescue her cat? Miss Menace.

Not the most flattering thing she had ever been called.

Not the worst, either.

"It has to be," Emmeline said. "No one was keen on murdering you before."

"Well, that's not exactly true," Priya said.

"Thank you for that," Sybil muttered.

"I imagine they have been keen on murdering us for quite some time. It's just as likely to be a result of any of a dozen things we have done, such as taking down the Marquess of Eastbourne. He no longer has his title, after all."

"Good," Sybil muttered. The shock of it had rippled through Mayfair.

"And Lord Portsmouth will hang."

"That's what you get for murdering your wives."

"Lady Solomon. Viscount Churleigh."

"The list is rather long," Sybil admitted. "And good for us. But honestly, a carriage coming out of a dark and rainy night could easily be a coincidence."

"I don't like it," Priya said.

"I'll be fine."

"Be *careful*."

"I always am."

The resounding snorts of doubt from every other woman in the room was rather rude, actually.

Apt, she was forced to admit. But rude all the same.

"The betting book has been useful already." Priya's dark hair gleamed in the sun struggling to shine through the early spring clouds. Her smile was sharp. Smug.

"It has?" Relief had Sybil taking a too-large gulp of hot tea. "How so?"

"As you know, we have been keeping an eye on several gentlemen of the *ton*. Many of them are members of the club and have placed bets."

"Anything incriminating?"

"A few of the regular sort of things to follow up on. But I did find something curious."

"Which is?" For Priya, something curious might be a discrepancy in the household ledgers or a secret message intercepted on its way to Napoleon. One could never be sure.

"These three tiny circles, overlapping and stacked up in a triangle formation," she explained, sketching one out with the pencil tied to her notebook with a silk ribbon.

"What does it mean?" Peony asked.

"I don't know yet."

"*You* don't know? That's alarming in itself."

"Eastbourne and Portsmouth both have the mark by their names in the betting book."

"And we already know they are terrible," Sybil said. "We helped prove it." Eastbourne had kept women with inheritances but no family captive in his cellar, and Portsmouth had had the regrettable habit of murdering his wives when they did not produce an heir.

Priya drummed her fingers on the table. "I should very much like to know who made these marks and why."

"A gentleman at the very least, if he is a member of Fortingham's," Sybil pointed out. "They are very picky about their membership and who crosses that sanctified threshold, present company not included."

"It's a start." Priya grinned. "Apparently, you were so bored you stole a case for us, Sybil."

"I do what I can." Sybil grinned back.

"Good, because there's more. I have a list here of all of those names with that symbol next to them, and I did a little digging."

"I know that tone." Peony dropped her toasted bread and leaned forward. "Do tell."

"The first is Lord St. John. He has three daughters, all out at fifteen. Two already betrothed. Reluctantly, it has to be said."

Matilda narrowed her eyes. "I know the nanny in that household. She is not fond of the parents. Either of them. Leave it to me."

"Excellent. And Lord Abbot. He tries to compromise young heiresses in the hopes of a rich marriage of necessity. Peony, would you take care of that, please?"

"I look forward to it. It will give me a chance to test out my new umbrella with the hidden sword."

"It's probably best not to skewer an earl if you can help it."

Peony pouted.

Sybil waited, her back teeth tensing.

"Sybil, I have left the Earl of Chiswick for you."

She let out a breath. "Thank God. If you told me to rest again I was going to stage a riot in your favorite parlor. The one with those giant ferns you love so much. It was going to be very messy. Not at all demure."

"I am aware."

"Is there mayhem involved? I find I am very much in the mood for mayhem." Anything to stop thinking about Keir and Violetta. About Keir at all. Though she already knew that was impossible.

"I need you to keep him distracted while we steal away his very unwilling bride. I sent word this morning, and she does not find that the age difference, as well as his syphilitic reputation, makes him an ideal marriage partner."

"He is ancient," Matilda confirmed. "And do let me guess— his newest bride is barely twenty."

"Seventeen."

Sybil stopped just short of rubbing her hands with glee. There was so much she could *not* do. She could not change Society's mind. She could not stop thinking about Keir's thighs and his green eyes and his soft-rough voice. But this was something she *could* do. Taking down an earl. She had done it before and she could do it again. "Is there a file on him?"

"Naturally." It was like asking if it rained in England. Priya slid the papers toward Sybil. "Feel free to leave your own mark."

"Even better."

Nothing quite like a nefarious plot to make a woman feel like herself again.

"Try not to get captured this time," Peony said.

Of course, friends had that effect as well.

"*One* time," Sybil said, sighing.

GAMING HELLS, MUCH like gentlemen's clubs, did not admit women.

Well, *ladies*.

As Sybil was both not enough of a lady and too much of a lady, she probably could have snuck in.

But it was so much more fun to arrive as Lord Singleton.

She loved dressing as a young lord with a cravat and breeches. She had chosen an eye-watering chartreuse for her waistcoat, to draw the eye away from her face. Not that anyone here was likely to recognize her, even if half a dozen of them had spoken to her in the last month. For one thing, they were far too drunk to notice much of anything.

Sybil *loved* pretending to be Lord Singleton. She had created him for just this purpose—to cross the drawbridge of places she could not attend as a woman. As herself. Fortingham's required membership, or she would have saved herself the social humiliation and stolen the betting book that way. But Lord Singleton could not apply for membership as he did not technically exist, nor did his viscount father living on the west coast of Ireland.

Still, Lord Singleton was very useful.

He could play vingt-et-un and billiards; he could walk wherever he wanted to without a companion. He could tell another gentleman to sod off. Which she did, with great enthusiasm, when he bumped into her on his way to the buffet table. She, in turn, bumped into a viscount and picked his pocket. Just for practice.

And fun.

Lord Singleton could also drink too much port (which she barely sipped and mostly spilled) and place wild wagers, all while egging on Lord Chiswick. The earl was repugnant. He had half a dozen bastards he did not support. It was a great pleasure to disrupt his plans and free Miss Maddox from his clutches, even if it meant choking on cheroot smoke and pretending to like port.

Say what you will, but the man could hold his liquor.

Regrettably.

She kept an eye on him as made a turn of the gaming rooms, ordering drinks for the others, playing a hand of vingt-et-un, beating Victor at billiards and grinning when he squinted as if he thought he recognized her from somewhere. More port wine.

How was it possible that Chiswick was not slumped over somewhere? The fumes coming from the man were enough to render her drunk just by standing downwind.

Still, she stayed close, trailing him from card table to side-board—for roast lamb—and back to the tables. She bet against him at whist and lost.

Then she bet against him again and won. A lot.

Just to keep his attention.

He could not, under any circumstances, go home. Not yet. Not until his bride-to-be was safely elsewhere. But how did a man of his advanced years drink half a bottle of brandy in the time it took for another to drink a single glass and barely weave on his feet? Sybil was faintly queasy just looking at him. He was meant to be unconscious by now. Not looking bored as he wiped his mouth and tossed his cards down.

"Is that all you've got?" he asked.

"Another game?"

"I've played every game in here and won. Bah." He stood up, motioning for his hat and coat. "Must get home. Getting married tomorrow, you know. A ripe little peach of a thing."

That would not do.

"Congratulations!" Sybil said heartily, instead of gagging, which was very much what she wanted to do. Especially when several men shouted encouragement at him.

"Get them while they are young and fresh!"

"May her cunny—"

Sybil did not hear the rest of the remark, as it ended in choked laughter and slaps on the back. She took note of it, though, and of every single man who shouted disrespectful comments. For later.

The Spinster Society kept a very detailed list.

For now, she passed Chiswick another bottle of brandy. This one had a pear suspended inside and glittered with gold leaf. "A toast to your lady!"

"To the delights of my marriage bed!"

He drank deep.

And still he kept to his feet.

Honestly, he ought to be studied by scientific academies. This very night, preferably.

This was not the way it was supposed to go. That much brandy was supposed to fell him, at which point Sybil would drag him into a distant closet and lock him inside. But Chiswick only accepted his beavery-crowned hat, his gold walking stick. Made another crude jest.

Plan B, then.

The earl's file indicated that he loved porkpies, brandy, and snuff. And that he was constitutionally unable to resist a horse race. And Sybil noticed that he did not seem to enjoy some of the comments about his lady, for vastly different reasons than Sybil disliked them. Chiswick glared far more pointedly at the younger men, the handsome, wealthy ones who were *not* old enough to be Miss Maddox's grandfather.

Sybil could use that.

The mark of a good Spinster was pivoting under pressure. Plan A gave way to Plan B, and often, Plan C. Sometimes D, E, and F.

She considered a duel, which would be fun, but it might be put off until the next day, and she did not fancy being shot at by an arthritic, syphilitic earl. She had much more experience with swords. He was old enough to prefer them.

She paused.

Too many variables.

A hit to the ego it was. At least she was unlikely to be locked in a cellar this time.

Sybil stood up and slammed her glass down in a great, loud display of dramatics. "I'm more interested in your actual filly, Chiswick!"

Chiswick frowned at her, though his curiosity was piqued. "Eh, lad?"

"I've heard she won at Newmarket."

"She did," he said, preening. "Twice."

"Wager that was blind luck," Sybil scoffed. "That was two years ago."

"Rode her myself to victory just last year at Prinny's party."

She snorted. "You couldn't keep your seat on him anymore."

Chiswick's eyes narrowed.

She had him.

"I wager I could beat *you*, insolent pup."

Someone whistled. A hand slapped on the table, the bet already taking life. They were drunk and bored, and horse racing was the ubiquitous Achilles heel of an English lord.

"It's a wager," Sybil said, smirking. "Let's have at it, then."

"Tomorrow. I've a wedding to prepare for."

She shook her head sadly. "That sounds too conveniently like doubt to me, Chiswick. Beat me now or not at all and know yourself to be a coward."

Someone hooted. Loudly.

"What do you say, Chiswick? A race in the Park before your

nuptials? Get the blood up, eh? You'll need it."

She knew that the earl, soused and desperate to seem young and virile, would not refuse. Could not.

Did not.

"Fine. Hurry up, then."

As far as Plan Bs went, it wasn't bad at all.

Until she spotted Keir. What was *he* doing here?

He was the sort to drink at home by the fire, to walk in the rain because it made you stronger. To pay court to ladies like Lady Violetta so they could have many babies to carry on the family name.

And, apparently, to ruin Sybil's night.

She forced herself to relax as she snuck glances in his direction. He did not belong here—he was steady as an anchor, the flotsam of the hell whirling around him.

But he would not notice her, and if he did, he certainly would not recognize her.

WHAT IN THE hell was Sybil Taunton doing in a gaming hell?

Keir had been asking himself what *he* was doing there for the last quarter of an hour, but this was a much more pressing question.

Sybil Taunton was swanning about the place in tight breeches, her tip-turned nose scattered with freckles. Her hair was tied back but it was still too shiny, too pretty. Like gold.

How had no one noticed that Lord Singleton was actually the very meddlesome, very pretty daughter of the Earl of Wentworth?

It strained credulity.

It was clearly not the first time she had done this. For one thing, when he had inquired over her presence, he was informed that Lord Singleton was a viscount's son from Ireland who liked to travel and buy rounds of port and wine and gin for everyone. He was well liked, even if no one could seem to recall a single relevant detail about his life.

For another thing, she was entirely too adept at moving about in those breeches, leaning over the billiards table so they tightened over her backside. She pitched her voice low as she loudly needled Chiswick into a horse race.

A bloody horse race at dawn in Hyde Park.

The woman was a menace to herself.

Surely she realized her disguise would fall away in tatters under the sunlight. It was one thing to pull such a ruse in a smoky, dimly lit gaming hell where the patrons were not exactly at their most observant.

And why pull such a ruse, in any case? Was it another trick that would land her in trouble, as the mess with Eastbourne had done? Something that might cause her to be nearly run down by a careless carriage driver again?

Like hell.

Like fucking hell.

There were many things he would like to do to Sybil that he could not.

Protecting her was not one of them.

CHAPTER NINE

S YBIL DID NOT care for carriage races. There were too many ways for the horses to sustain injuries. If a drunken lord broke his own leg or even his neck, that was his problem. The human idiots could live with the consequences. The horses should not have to.

But a simple horse race?

That was so much better than cards or dancing or climbing trellises. The bite of the wind on her cheeks, the slap of the horse's hooves and the bellows of his breath as they worked together to the same purpose.

Beating the Earl of Chiswick and buying Miss Maddox more time.

And for once, it wasn't raining.

Mostly because it was snowing instead. A beautiful, soft snow, just starting to fall. The ground was hard and packed, not yet wet or icy. It would not turn slick and dangerous for some time. It clung to the bare branches of lilac trees and linden trees and giant, shaggy oaks, to streetlamps and shop windows. It gleamed and glittered under a sky glowing pink and clementine.

There were worse ways to spend a too-early morning.

Half of the gaming hell poured out of the doors and rushed to jump into carriages, all heading toward Hyde Park. A horse race, a pot of coffee, and a wedding.

Well, not the wedding part.

Sybil would have smirked if she wasn't currently trying to figure out how to race a horse without an actual horse.

Plan B needed some work, apparently.

She'd forgotten that not only had she taken a hackney to keep her identity secret, but even if she had not, neither her father's horses nor Priya's could offer Chiswick enough of a challenge. He'd win the race before she'd even convinced her horse to consider a trot.

Bollocks.

She didn't have much time. There was a big, strong-looking horse just at the corner, but a groom held his reins and he did not look friendly. Or short enough that she could cosh him on the head and steal the beast.

"You're thinking of stealing my horse."

Keir.

His voice was soft and knowing, and right behind her. The warmth of him blocked the wind for a moment. Of course the horse belonged to him. He needed something sturdy enough to handle a giant. She should have guessed.

Why was he still here? Surely horse races were beneath him.

She angled her face away just in case, even though he would never recognize her.

"Sybil," he said, patiently. Pointedly.

Her mouth dropped open and she whirled on him. "*What?*"

"I know it's you."

"Shh!" She tugged the brim of her hat a little lower in case anyone had overheard him, even though he was very soft spoken for a man who looked like he could shout the trees down.

He continued to look down at her, inscrutable as always. Maybe not *quite* as inscrutable. She was fairly certain there was a tiny muscle twitching by his left eyebrow. "You cannot have my horse," he said.

She frowned. "I need him more than you do."

"Like you needed the betting book?"

"Precisely. And will you hush? You are not very good at sub-terfuge, are you, my lord?"

"I've never had the occasion to take on another name and character, no."

"Pity."

"Pity?"

"It's amusing." She shrugged. "And you could do with some amusement," she added in a mutter under her breath.

He loomed over her, but she felt sheltered instead of intimi-dated. She wondered if that would shock him. "What are you doing, Sybil?"

She adjusted her gloves the way she had seen countless young men do. "I'm getting ready to win a horse race."

"Let me try again," he said, clearly growing more exasperated by the second. Good. She hated when he was all lordly and controlled. The infamously calm Lord Blackburn destroyed his enemies both at home, in Parliament, and on the Continent with cold, brutal efficiency.

She preferred Keir. This was the man who had dared to show his sense of humor in a note written after midnight.

"*Why* are you trying to win a horse race which you clearly baited an old man into taking?" he pressed.

"That old man is goat dung."

"No argument there. But I won't be distracted, Sybil."

Why did he keep saying her name? It was too intimate, too personal. Private. She liked the sound of it too much in his mouth. "I don't owe you any explanations."

"You do if you want my horse."

"It was very considerate of you to bring him for me."

"I think you mean coincidental." Now he looked as though he was trying not to be amused. *Finally.*

"*Very* considerate," she said.

"Sybil." A warning this time.

One she had no intention of heeding. Obviously.

Especially not when another wave of drunken patrons stumbled through the doors behind them, clogging the pavement. Very convenient.

Very convenient, indeed.

Keir was stronger.

But Sybil was faster.

She tossed him a grin over her shoulder and darted into the crowd. He bellowed her name. Better yet, he was considerate enough to bellow her assumed name. "Singleton, damn it!"

She decided she was terribly fond of him right then and there.

"Bates," he called to his groom. "Keep tight to those reins."

Perhaps not *that* fond.

Sybil reached the groom long before Keir. Bates frowned at the crowd of stumbling lords, the traffic of carriages and horses suddenly surging away from the hell. He was tall, clearly competent. The horse was well cared for and a veritable beast.

But neither of them were prepared for Sybil.

Which was exactly how she liked it. People were always so much more obliging when she took them by surprise.

She caught his gaze and smiled. "Lord Blackburn has been kind enough to lend me his horse." She kept her voice light, natural, nearly cloying in its debutante sweetness. *Ha.* Debutantes were as sweet as unripe lemons. But it did the job.

He blinked at her. "Miss?"

"You wouldn't put a lady in danger, would you?" It was technically true. Sybil might not be in danger, but Miss Maddox most assuredly was.

She did not wait for a reply, merely leapt into the saddle (so much easier in breeches!). The groom was still blinking after the sudden appearance of a madwoman in breeches as she urged the horse into a careful trot, Keir's curses blistering the air behind them.

DAWN GLOWED BEHIND the veils of snow slowly draping over Hyde Park. It was like being inside a meringue, all light and softness. Birds sang from the white branches. It took Sybil some time to reach a section of the path wide enough for a race. Spectators crowded along the side, breath misting above them as they complained about the weather and passed flasks of whisky back and forth.

She pulled her beast of a horse up next to the earl, eyeing him sharply. He was not entirely sober, but he was steady and was not likely to injure his horse in the process of the race. Nor hers. If he landed on his own backside and broke it in two, she would be the first to cheer.

"See if you can keep your seat, old man," she taunted him, grinning. He could not back out now. Sybil needed to buy more time. As Spinster House might no longer be as safe as it should be, they would need a little more time to find Miss Maddox a safer place to hide.

Chiswick muttered something she could not hear.

"Go on, Chiswick!" someone shouted. "Show this upstart what you're made of!"

She patted her horse's neck. "You are a lovely beast. All we need to do is gallop for a bit. Nothing fancy." He tossed his mane once. "Yes, you're very handsome."

She had no idea if he was fast. If the earl's horse was fast. It did not matter. One learned to swallow one's pride in the name of misdirection and subterfuge.

Oh, but it would be nice to win.

Someone had produced a red knitted scarf and sacrificed it to the cause. A gentleman held each end, stretching across the path.

"First to reach the twisted oaks wins!" He paused. "What's the prize?"

"Glory!"

"Glory it is!" The gentleman paused again, this time with great flair. "Are you ready?"

"Just have at it, man!" Chiswick bellowed.

"I guess he's ready," the gentleman muttered.

Sybil leaned down over her horse's neck. "You are saving a lady this fine morning. Try not to toss me out of the saddle, if you please."

The scarf billowed up, tauntingly, back down, up again—and was released, finally dropping into the snow.

The race was on.

Sybil laughed into the wind as she held on for dear life. The cold whistled in her hair. The snow was like wet fingers under the collar. The weather was not salubrious. But the horse did not care. And she did not care.

Chiswick cared. He cursed and squinted into the air, hat long gone. It had landed in a tree some meters back.

Her horse thundered on, and she let him take the lead. His mane tickled her nose as she leaned down. Mud and slush flew from under his hooves.

Behind her, Chiswick bounced around in his saddle. His gloves were no match for the weather. His expression suggested he had been eating lemons. With salt. In vinegar.

It was glorious.

So was winning.

When Sybil finally slid out of the saddle, her cheeks were red, her fingers cramped, her boots muddy, her heart thundering in her chest. In other words: she was happy.

Even when the cold threatened to turn into something with teeth. Something made from memory and iron and a cellar. If the sun could make a valiant effort to shine through the clouds, so could she.

Someone clapped her on the shoulder in congratulations as he passed by and nearly sent her headfirst into a tree. Keir caught her by the back of her coat and righted her. "You could have been killed, damn it."

"By a tree?" A more reasonable person might have started with an apology for stealing his horse. Maybe placated him a little. Not her usual tactics.

"Not that, and you know it."

She raised her brows. "In a horse race?" Now that was mildly insulting.

"In a race on a horse you do not know and in the snow. You could have been injured."

When he put it like *that*, it did not sound as much fun. Necessary but, very well, possibly reckless, even for her. Not that she would ever admit to it. Certainly not to him. "But I *wasn't* injured."

"You could have injured my horse."

She sucked in a breath, truly offended for the first time. "I would *never*."

He studied her for a long moment before frowning. It was much frownier than the one he used for her fake swooning and horse racing and general havoc. "You're cold." It was downright accusatory.

"It's winter." She studied him for a moment. He did not look cold at all. Only cross. And something else she could not decipher. "I did not take you for the type to frequent a gaming hell until dawn."

"And here I took you entirely for that type."

Was that an insult? A compliment?

She would jump naked into the Thames before asking.

"What were you doing, Sybil?"

"Hush!" She poked him hard.

"Everyone is dispersing. There's no one near enough to hear me."

He was right. She hadn't noticed. It was hard to notice anything but him.

Which was embarrassing, really. After all this time.

The others were indeed huddling back into the warmth of their waiting carriages, exchanging winnings. Chiswick was being helped discreetly off his horse. He looked sore. *Ha.* Served him right.

She considered running and tackling him to the ground. Challenging him to that duel. Pushing him into the Serpentine. But she had done all that she could do. Now she could only trust that the others had spirited Miss Maddox away already. She was due for her marriage ceremony in an hour.

Keir sighed when he realized that not only was Sybil not going to give him an explanation but was already distracted by something else. His mouth twitched as if he were fighting a smile, but his tone was dry as dust. "Horse thievery is a hanging offense."

"Only if you're caught."

"I caught you."

She nearly asked him what he planned to do with her now that he had caught her, but bit her tongue instead. They did not talk about that. Ever.

Proof she could control herself. Make rational decisions.

Which was about as diverting as *resting*.

She grimaced inwardly and tried to take the reasonable route after one steals a horse, wins a race, and is caught in the snow in borrowed breeches.

Retreat.

"Thank you for your assistance, Lord Blackburn." She bowed sharply, more than a little tauntingly. She had to bite her back teeth down as she fought a full-body shiver. The snow was hitting the back of her neck again and also seeping into her shoes. She needed to get home and get warm. *Now.* "Goodnight."

His fingers closed over her wrist. "I think the hell not."

Her eyes widened. "Such language, *Lord Blackburn.*"

"Get in the carriage, *Miss Taunton.*"

"I can walk home."

He did not move, did not release her wrist. Did not blink as he studied her. "No."

She thought about fighting him just for the fun of it, but there was very little fun in trudging home with icy toes that might shatter if they got any colder. "Fine." She climbed the step. "But don't get any ideas, Lord Blackburn—I cannot marry you," she said, echoing his words from the night she pilfered the betting book.

For some reason, his jaw clenched. She fancied she could hear his molars grinding together.

She felt quite cheerful after all, despite the cold.

He had hired a hackney, no doubt while still cursing her name. Bates had already come to claim the horse. The carriage was warm and cozy, and with Keir, it felt considerably smaller. He propped his boot against the door with a raised eyebrow, referring to the fact that she had run away the minute his back was turned the last time he had popped her into a carriage. "You don't trust me?" she asked.

"I *know* you."

But why should he mind that she had slipped away from the Willoughby ball, aside from a bit of concern? She had done him a favor, surely. He was not fond of messiness, and she was nothing if not messy.

But he did not look inclined to let her go at the moment.

And she did not want him to.

That was a problem.

She bit back a sigh, could not bite back a shiver. The snow had melted through her coat and her stockings, clammy and chill. The warm brick at her feet was absolutely heaven but not quite enough to battle the weather she had dragged in with her.

Keir scowled. She was no doubt dripping all over the floors, staining the seats, which, at least, were not the fancy ones of his personal carriage. There was mud on her boots. Why was there always mud all over her when he was around?

"You're still cold," he said darkly. As if it offended him to his very soul.

"I'm not." Her teeth chattered around the lie.

He cursed. "You're soaked through, you little liar."

"Just a bit." When he reached for her legs, she blinked at him. "What are you doing?"

"Getting you warm, since you seem incapable of staying out of the cold like any reasonable person."

"I had a job to do."

"Catch your death?"

"No, stop a wedding."

He pulled off her boots and then undid the buttons at the knees of her breeches, while she watched, not knowing if she should do it herself, not wanting him to stop. His hands were big and warm and exceedingly gentle as he rolled down her wet stockings. He cursed at the sight of her bare calves, mottled pink with cold. The scars on her ankle looked angry. She tugged away slightly, embarrassed despite knowing better than to care about such things. Her head knew the scars were just scars. Other parts of her wanted to be warm and smooth and pretty when Keir was looking at her.

"Stay still," he ordered her. He stroked his palms up and down her calves, rubbing very gently to warm her up. He did not seem satisfied with the results and plucked her out of her seat instead, as though she were a great deal smaller than she was, tucking her into his side. "Take off your coat."

Dazed, she obeyed. He pulled her under his coat, against his chest, the place she loved the most even when she wanted to poke him repeatedly with a sharp stick. He was so warm and sturdy and smelled so nice, with a hint of snow. "Why is it you're always warming me up?"

"Why is it you don't know better than to traipse around London in the dead of night in winter?"

"Extenuating circumstances."

"I am beginning to think your entire life is an extenuating circumstance."

She smiled softly. "Sometimes it does feel that way."

"You have to have more care." He said it softly, less a command, more a plea. As if it truly did matter to him.

"I'm not fragile, Keir. It's just a bit of cold." But it wasn't, not since the cellar. She had come too close to *that* kind of cold again, the one that clawed icy fingers into her chest and would not let go.

Except Keir made it let go.

Somehow, he made it let go.

It wasn't just that he was so solid and exuded warmth like a bonfire. It was something else. Something purely *Keir*.

And for now, it was hers.

A single, quiet moment in a carriage trundling through quiet snowy streets. Warmth and darkness and safety.

And Keir's mouth.

CHAPTER TEN

K ISSING KEIR WAS a much, *much* nicer way to warm up.

He was the spark of a Yule log, the burn of whisky, a lightning strike on midsummer. How could he be all of these wild and primal things and still the Marquess Blackburn with his unwavering adherence to duty and honor and not-smiling was beyond her.

There was nothing of duty in this kiss.

It was desperate.

Forbidden.

Necessary.

And it burned through her from the top of her head to the tips of her frozen toes. It melted away the cold, the knowledge that this changed nothing, as always. None of that mattered. Not with his hand cradling her nape, digging into the stiff muscles there, twisting in her hair. Not with the soft groan that rumbled in his chest as though she were the sweetest of sweets. As though each taste was the first.

She made sounds of her own, a gasp, a moan. Very nearly a whimper just from the slide of his tongue against hers. It was a deep, slow kiss, one that had every intention of rewriting every single thing she thought she knew about her body. She felt it in her belly, in her thighs, in her ribcage. In the dark corners of her mind where every worry sat waiting for her to let down her guard. She was too much, her curves were too soft, her laugh too loud. None of that mattered. None of it even existed.

She kissed him back, nipping at his lower lip, sucking it into her mouth until his fingers tightened in her hair and he muttered something lovely and filthy.

Not at all the kind of poetry one might expect from the Marquess Blackburn.

As a rule, they did not speak of what burned between them. Not even as it burned between them. But the things he whispered to her now made her thighs clench.

He was Keir, the real Keir that she sometimes thought she saw beneath the inscrutable mask. And then he dragged kisses across her jaw and sucked at the spot below her ear and every single remaining thought fled from her. Every single one. Mere words were left: *more, please. Again.*

There was only the hard press of his chest against hers as he held her closer, the tightening of her nipples in response. The light scrape of his teeth, his tongue soothing the spot. The arousal pooling throughout her body and making her feel like she were as pliant as melting beeswax all honey and fire.

It was everything. Too much. Not enough.

It would never be enough.

He slipped his hand inside her breeches, sliding his fingers between her already slick and swollen folds. "You're so wet for me," he murmured as though she had pleased him.

He never spoke like this. It did things to her she could not have expected. It made her feel soft and feral, all whimpering breath but also teeth. *"Keir."*

Saying his name seemed to unlock something in him. The intensity of his gaze burned through her, licked up her spine, tingled through her thighs. He curled two fingers inside her passage, using his thumb to tease her bud, circling it slowly, then flicking over it until she gasped. She arched against him, desperate for more. Her leg muscles quivered as she chased the press of his hand, squirming away at the same time when it was too much.

She rode him until her vision sparked, until the pleasure tightened and sharpened inside her.

He bit into her neck and the waves crested immediately, crashing through her.

The ferociousness of it did not ease. She ripped the buttons of his own breeches open, and he sprang free into her palm, hot and silky and hard. She gripped him, not gently, pumping up and down until his breaths were ragged and harsh. He yanked her breeches down, dragging her over his lap, her knees on either side. His fingers dimpled in the curve of her hips. "Ride me, Sybil. Use me."

The sound of his husky voice was devastating. She fitted him at her opening and then eased down, agonizingly slow, torturing them both. When she was seated, filled to the hilt, she rolled her hips. He jerked up into her, shooting sensations through limbs. She pulled up, dropped back down. His forehead was pressed to her throat and she clung to him, met each movement with a thrust. Her legs burned. He surged up, grasping her waist and taking control, lifting her easily, sliding her back down over his cock until she moaned, intimate muscles fluttering in response.

He gritted his teeth, refusing to come until she collapsed against him, shaking and whimpering. He surged up again, then pulled out and groaned, spending into a handkerchief.

It took some time for Sybil to catch her breath. She was feeling too much.

She pulled her clothes back on and shoved her feet into her wet boots. And then the sun finally won its battle with the wintry clouds and pierced through the gaps in the curtains. It was too bright and too warm and too real.

When she had put herself back to rights, the carriage pulled to a stop.

Keir helped her down without a word.

She darted up the steps to Spinster House, also without a word.

And she quite forgot to ask how he knew where she lived

when she was not at home.

SYBIL FOUND HERSELF in the Park later that afternoon, after a very few hours of sleep.

Mostly because one could not spend *every* moment reliving a tryst in a hired hackney. No matter how it threatened to sear into one's soul and remain there forever.

Something had changed. Was changing. Maybe?

But just because *she* could not stop thinking about it, that did not mean that Keir was similarly affected. She mostly elicited an exasperated stare or the enthusiasm of a stone from him.

When they weren't clawing at each other, all desperate mouths and hands.

A hot tingle raced through her, unbidden, ungovernable.

It had been like that since she woke. Tea had not helped, nor toasted bread, nor throwing knives at a target in the ballroom. A bracing walk would surely do the trick. The sky was a hard shell of blue, sunlight glistening on the icy glass of the Serpentine and the mounds of fresh snow. Children ran past with red woolen mittens and matching red cheeks, shouting with unrestrained glee. Ladies promenaded in their thickest pelisses, hands warm in fur muffs. A cart offering roasted chestnuts and gingerbread in paper wraps did brisk business. It was cheerful and crowded, everyone taking advantage of the sun's brief appearance, of the storybook snow turning London into a soft confection.

Sybil bought her own bag of peeled chestnuts and popped one into her mouth. It was sweet and warm and perfectly brought to mind Christmas outings to gather holly and pine boughs from Hyde Park, even though it was frowned upon. The tip of her nose was cold and the rest of her pleasantly warm. She skirted a snowball battle and three snow angels.

Couples walked closer than was generally considered appropriate, taking advantage of the cold. They sat on benches and shared gingerbread. They wandered into the trees for a moment of romantic privacy.

"They" suddenly included Sophie and a young gentleman Sybil did not recognize.

She paused as he whispered something in Sophie's ear. Sophie blushed.

Sybil did not wish to break up a lovely stolen moment.

Except that something in her belly tightened in warning.

And she had learned to trust herself, despite the fact that her body now reacted to the cold as though she were in danger. She would not let Eastbourne's cellar steal that from her. Not when Sophie's reputation might be at stake. Damn her reputation—her safety was paramount.

Sybil strode forward, pasting on her most cheerful smile. No need to make a fuss and embarrass the girl. At her age, Sybil would have been mortified if an older woman had interrupted with well-meaning lectures.

An older woman.

A spinster.

Sybil struggled not to let her smile turn into a disgruntled sigh.

If she was going to be a dried-up, wizened old spinster at the age of twenty-nine, then let it be for some good.

"Sophie," she said calmly.

"Sybil!" Sophie started, eyes widening guiltily. "Is my brother with you?"

"No, why should he be?" Sybil would not think on that answer too hard.

"Oh, good." Sophie wilted with relief. Her cheeks were pink. She looked as fetching a young girl with her first secret love could ever look. "Miss Taunton, may I present Mr. Pelham."

"Good afternoon," Sybil greeted him neutrally. Politely. And with a narrowed eye. She could not help herself. Something about him set off internal bells.

"Miss Taunton." He bowed with a charming grin. His hair curled over his forehead and into his eyes, also charming. He tossed it clear, charmingly.

He was charmingly charming.

Sybil nearly groaned. *Blast.* She did not trust charming. And she recognized his name from Priya's list of known fortune hunters.

Blast *and* botheration.

"Mr. Pelham, was it? I knew your father."

It was a bland, nothing statement that said everything. She knew his father had cut him off, which meant she also knew he had been caught trying to steal away to Gretna Green with a young girl just last month. His smile slipped, then dazzled brighter. "How do you know my father?"

"Miss Taunton is the daughter of Lord Wentworth," Sophie put in.

"I know a great many people." Sybil smiled back, just as dazzling, only hers was the dazzle of a sharpened knife, not a paste jewel.

"I see." He took Sophie's hand. "Miss Montgomery, I have taken too much of your time." She blushed. He turned to Sybil, who met his eyes squarely, without a word. "Erm. Miss Taunton."

They watched him hurry through the snow. Sophie bounced on her toes once. "Isn't he too handsome?"

"He is very pretty. He is a bit older than you."

"He is only twenty-four."

"I see. Why is he not courting a debutante?"

"He says they are dull as ditchwater. He says I am not like the other girls."

"Does he now."

Sophie grimaced. "Oh, not that tone."

"Tone?"

"'Sophie, you're too young. Sophie, you're too reckless.' The *Keir* tone. I thought you different."

Sybil raised an eyebrow. "I *am* different, Sophie. Which is why I will tell you I do not begrudge you a flirtation."

"You... don't?"

"But I will also point out that being like other girls should not be an insult."

"Oh." Sophie frowned. "I suppose not."

"And I will add that if you choose to sneak about without your chaperone and with a man that your brother has not vetted, then you must be far more clever than you are being at present."

Sophie blinked at her. "You are never sharp with me."

"This is important."

"It was only a kiss." She wrinkled her nose. "Or three."

"Kisses are lovely and do not concern me."

"They don't?" She clearly was not expecting that response.

"No, as I said, what concerns me is *you*."

"My reputation."

"Certainly. Reputations are a tiresome thing, but they are one of the very few weapons we have. Usually, they are turned against us, but if we are very clever, we can wield them for ourselves."

Sophie had stopped staring after Mr. Pelham. "This is not the kind of lecture my governess ever gave me."

"I expect not, so listen to me carefully, if you please." Sybil really ought to start a finishing school of her own, for girls on the cusp of becoming debutantes. To teach them the important things. Investigation. Subterfuge. How to use a sharp bonnet pin to discourage unwanted advances.

"Did you see his boots?" Sybil asked even though she knew perfectly well that Sophie had paid no attention whatsoever to his boots.

"What of them?"

"They are far better quality than his hat. That is because hats are flashy. It is a simple thing to steal one or buy one cheaply from a valet replacing his master's wardrobe. Even a good theater company can make a hat passable for a stroll through Mayfair. But Hessian boots are terribly expensive. And they make you *look* expensive, especially if you are a fortune hunter who has been cut off but are still pretending to be flush."

"You can't know that from a hat and a pair of boots."

"I can know that and more from a great many small details. And so can you."

Sophie lifted her chin defiantly, but she was still frowning. "He said he loved me."

"And I hope he does. But as a debutante with a large dowry, it is best you know how to spot these things for yourself whenever possible."

"My brother would never marry me off to a fortune hunter."

Sybil thought of Keir's quiet, intense gaze. The set of his jaw at the thought of a lady not being warm enough. "He would not. But wouldn't you rather know for yourself?"

"I suppose I would."

"Sometimes, you can't," Sybil said. "I'll be honest about that. Sometimes we get fooled. But why make it easy for them?"

Sophie nodded thoughtfully as they walked through the snow back to the main path. "No one has ever told me anything like this."

"I know. Perhaps I ought to tell you to talk to your brother or some such thing instead. But the reason fortune hunters can talk girls into eloping—or into other, more unsavory things—is because we insist on treating them like they are dolls."

"I am *not* a doll."

"Then allow me to also tell you that your Mr. Pelham tried to elope with a Miss Aldridge just last month."

Sophie's mouth dropped open. "He met me *two* months ago! In the village near my school." She huffed out a breath. "Where Miss Aldridge used to attend, by the way."

"I expect he was in that particular village by design, then."

Sophie crossed her arms, vexed. Clearly also hurt, but mostly vexed. "That... arse."

"I am sorry, Sophie. Are you in love with him?"

"I liked him very much, but now I wish equally as much to kick him very hard in the shins."

"Two things can be true at once." Sybil smiled. "I can teach you how to kick to best effect without breaking your own toes."

"Good." Sophie's eyes were swimming with tears, but she did not let them fall. "I should like to marry one day. Not him, obviously. I was never going to *marry* him. But are you saying I cannot? Should not? Ever?"

"Certainly not," Sybil said. "This isn't about love or matches made with clear, honest eyes whatever their private agreements might be. This is about power and respect and unscrupulous people. That is all."

"And you won't tell my brother?"

"If you'll promise me you'll be more careful." Telling Keir would only result in a row. And several more chaperones, possibly an armed guard. All of which would only have made Sybil dig in her heels and rebel all the harder at the age of sixteen. Sophie might well elope out of spite. "And you will take my suggestions to your friends. I will give you a list of peers to avoid, and their families. Some of those fortune hunters' mothers are far worse, believe me."

Sophie smiled grimly. "This is much more useful than any French lessons or my abysmal watercolors."

Sybil knew what it felt like to be overlooked, to be trapped, to be grateful and happy and not care about what others thought of you while still somehow caring what others thought of you. It was exhausting. Stifling. "Your first lesson?" she asked, gathering snow in her mittens.

"Yes?"

"Practice your aim—you never know when it might come in handy."

Sybil proceeded to hit her square in the face with the snowball.

Sophie squawked. Snow dripped from her chin. "You..." she sputtered. She shivered when a splatter of water snuck under her scarf. "This means war!"

Sybil laughed. "Make me proud!"

The resulting volleys of snowballs would have made a master

gunner proud. Snow flew, as did insults and shouts and screams of laughter. A few passersby sniffed in disdain, but many more smiled. Several children joined the war. Sybil crouched, throwing snowball after snowball until she was breathless with laughter. Sophie finally hid behind a tree, hair damp, smile wide. "I yield!"

But Sybil still had a snowball in her possession. And it was perfect. Soft, well formed, ready to fly. She considered it carefully.

Sophie pointed to her left, where the reasonable members of Society promenaded and stopped to greet each other. They were dry and fashionable and not at all sweaty and messy. They were like Keir.

Just like Keir, in fact.

Standing there, large as a standing stone, with his dark hair and his strong shoulders and perfect posture. Sybil would know him anywhere, even from the back. His coat was dark blue, cut simply. His hair curled, just a bit at his nape, under his beaver-crown hat. He looked nothing like the man who had taken her in a carriage just that morning.

Sophie waggled her eyebrows.

Sybil, never able to refuse a challenge or a really bad idea, took aim.

Her perfect snowball arced over the heads of fascinated children, a dog with long, floppy ears, an older woman eating a peppermint candy.

And then it hit Keir squarely in the back of the head.

Sophie positively crowed with laughter.

Keir turned slowly, and when his eyes met Sybil's, he did not seem even a little surprised to see her.

Lady Violetta, however, was.

She had been blocked by Keir's towering body, her lilac pelisse rimmed with white fur to match her muff. Her rosebud mouth made a moue of surprise. Her eyes twinkled with a giggle under the brim of her bonnet.

Sophie darted toward her big brother, flushed and happy and thinking not at all about Mr. Pelham, and that made it worthwhile. Made the sour worm inside Sybil's chest easier to ignore. The one that said, once again, that she was too wild, too impulsive. Too much.

Always too much when she was not pretending to be a wallflower, a young lord, a fine lady lost in the rain.

When she was herself.

Especially when faced with someone who was just right.

Sybil had been jealous before, of course. One did not grow up without wrestling with some unbecoming emotions. When she was very little, she had been jealous of the sea for keeping her father away for so long. Later, of the bigger children for being able to muscle closer to the fire barrels. Of people who walked right into bakeries and bought whatever they liked. After Amandine brought her home, her rare jealousy was reserved for country house parties or Parliament, which claimed her parents for long hours or days at a time.

It was humbling to be jealous of a woman who had done nothing wrong and who was, indeed, the wronged party from any angle. Lady Violetta was kind and patient and had a sense of humor. She also had Keir as a suitor.

While Sybil was digging snow out of her ear, put there by a little boy missing his front teeth, Lady Violetta was strolling daintily, her hand around Keir's muscular forearm.

Sybil was quite sure that Lady Violetta had never assaulted a peer of the realm with a snowball to the back of the head.

Because Sybil suddenly felt odd and awkward and did not care for it one whit, she curtsied at the couple with a cheeky and wholly unrepentant smile.

And then she hurried home, head held high, eyes stinging from the cold.

CHAPTER ELEVEN

WHILE THROWING SNOWBALLS at Keir's head was surprisingly entertaining, there was work to do.

Sybil was grateful for it, as it might afford her an afternoon to not embarrass herself in front of the *ton*. Although, given her record, she was not particularly hopeful.

Spinster House took in mostly debutantes and widows and heiresses, but there was another house in Covent Garden that took in maids and prostitutes and fishwives and watercress sellers. They shared information between them and occasionally traded hideaways for those who needed the extra security of an entirely unfamiliar neighborhood. Between them was the Golden Griffin bookshop, which facilitated communication.

It was also known for its vast collections of works written by women. As well as the naughtier tomes, which lent it a certain kind of reputation that mostly resulted in rotten vegetables thrown at the window.

That was until the proprietress, Miss Kitty Caldecott, had married the Devil. Devil, also known as the Earl of Birmingham, owned a gaming hell and half the debts of the most powerful people in London. No one dared cross him. He was as feared as Priya.

They did not get along.

But Kitty was an honorary member of the Spinster Society,

despite a rocky beginning. She also kept late hours for the purpose of offering help to those who might not be comfortable venturing into Mayfair to seek out the Spinsters directly.

The bookshop ceiling was a moody blue and accented with gilded griffins, from one so large it nearly spanned the length to another so small you had to know where it was to find it at all. It was a safe place, just like Spinster House.

When the brass bell attached to the front door rang, Kitty emerged from the back room, carrying a stack of books. Her red hair was a riot of curls escaping their pins. "Sybil, have you read through those books I sent you already?"

"I was confined to my chambers for two days."

"Ghastly."

"Exceedingly. And they are all still after me to rest, rest, rest."

"Monsters."

"My thoughts exactly. So I thank you for those novels. They were not at all morally improving."

Kitty grinned. "Good."

"But this time, I am afraid I am here on Spinster business."

"Ah. Tea?"

"Yes, please. You have the best tea. Don't tell Priya I said so."

"When I found a favorite one, Devil bought a crate for the shop and two for the house."

"A wise man."

Kitty snorted.

"Clever, then," Sybil amended with a grin. He was also ruthless and unforgiving. A thump sounded from above, rattling the chandelier. She glanced up. "Should I be worried?"

"We are turning the second floor into a proper lending library. With more than one chair." The shop was not large. The library was even smaller. "And by we, I mean that Devil sent men with hammers and drawings for me to approve."

"Very clever, indeed."

"If I don't let him do these things, he buys me *jewelry*," Kitty grumbled as if she had just said he sent her dead fish. "He bought diamond buckles for my shoes. And he *almost* bought me a jeweled hairbrush." She grimaced. "Ridiculous."

"Never mind clever, the man is *brilliant*." Sybil sat down while Kitty brought over a plate of gingerbread and marzipan shaped like hedgehogs. Kitty's sister had spent some time at Spinster House with her pet hedgehog Galahad. Sybil missed them both. "You would have fought him over the shop improvements, which was what he actually wanted to give you, so he distracted you with other things."

"He's Machiavellian," Kitty agreed. "And he's so handsome, too. It's quite disgusting."

"Truly diabolical. I can see that you are suffering."

Kitty popped a hunk of gingerbread into her mouth, her eyes twinkling. Marriage to a notorious man suited her. "So, what can I do for you?"

Sybil pulled the paper from her reticule and laid it on the table.

"What's this?"

"I was hoping you could tell me."

Kitty unfolded the paper and glared at the symbol of three circles. "I've seen this before. Or I've heard of it, anyway."

Sybil perked up. Finally, a *clue*. "You have?"

"A viscount's son came to tell me he had been associated with a new society of gentlemen by this mark. He was most offended."

"A society," Sybil murmured, mind racing. "That makes sense."

"Why? Where did you hear of them?"

"We found this symbol in the Fortingham betting book, next to a list of names we have since discovered are not particularly honorable. And someone has been targeting the Spinsters ever since. Warnings, mostly."

"Priya warned me as well," Kitty said. "And then Devil added two guards. I really do have my own army now. But there's been nothing out of the ordinary. At least, not here."

"That's something at least. And between him and Priya, this

society business has no chance of success," Sybil said smugly. But not as smugly as she would have liked. Her fellow Spinsters were in danger.

"Still. Be careful."

"Why does everyone keep saying that to me?"

"Because we have met you. Have another marzipan."

"Are *you* being careful?" Kitty was as reckless as Sybil.

"I have my own army, remember?"

"Fair enough. Any idea who might be in charge of this little society?"

"I'm afraid not. I only know as much as I do because I helped that viscount's son once."

Sybil nodded. "Thank you. It's still more than we had this morning." She set down her cup. "We knew it could not be coincidence. Priya will be pleased. She is going to send you so much tea, you might need a third floor."

ON SYBIL'S WAY home, she was grabbed off the street.

Right off the busy street. In the middle of the afternoon.

She tried to bite her attacker and got cuffed on the ear for her trouble. By the time she had reached for her hatpin, it was too late. There was a sack over her head that smelled like stale oats and her arm was viciously wrenched behind her back. Fear made her mouth dry, her pulse thunder. She tried to breathe slowly, to keep the panic from taking her over.

Her knees dug into the floor of the carriage. There were at least two captors and very little space to move between them. The wheels creaked over a deep rut and her bones rattled when she was tossed to the side. She cursed. Viciously.

One of the men whistled. "Listen to the mouth on this one."

"Let me go at once," she snapped. "I do not have a dowry, so you are wasting your time."

A snort. "No one wants to marry *you*."

"Oh, that is a relief." She kept her tone calm and dry, even though her heart threatened to fill her throat. She jabbed her elbow back as hard as she could. There was a grunt when she connected with someone's thigh.

It was a short-lived victory, as he shoved her hard into the door.

"We're just seeing you home, lovey. Streets aren't safe. Thieves about, don't you know?"

"What is this about?" She refused to gasp, even though her shoulder had hit the metal handle with some force.

"Just a friendly warning."

"As there is no such thing, you may take your friendly warning and shove it directly—"

Another shove to cut her off.

"He said you'd say something like that."

Keep calm. You're a Spinster, for God's sake.

"Who said that?" she asked.

"None of your business. Now shut your gob."

"This is a warning," the other man said. "If you're smart, you'll mind yourself. Stop poking into the affairs of men. No more betting books."

Sybil laughed. She could not help it.

The other captor made a sound in the back of his throat, half impressed. "She's cracked."

"Last warning, girl."

"I doubt that very much."

"Minos didn't tell us—"

"Shut your face, Alfie."

Minos.

Alfie.

It was something. Another piece of the puzzle. She would take it.

As well as the pause, the slip in concentration when Alfie said more than he was supposed to. That was even better.

Since Sybil was already pressed against the door, it was easy enough to kick out as she grabbed for the handle.

Tumbling out of a moving carriage in London was not wise.

But it was wiser than staying where she was.

She only had that one moment, that fleeting element of surprise, and she would use it. She had no idea if they planned to release her or if they had something else in mind, and she had no intention of finding out.

There was a shout, a flurry of movement when the door popped open.

Sybil threw herself out, tucking her shoulder and hoping she was not about to be trampled by another carriage. Or break her leg. Crack her skull.

She hit the ground hard, and it knocked the breath right out of her. She yanked at the sack over her head. She had hit the edge of the cobbles, mostly out of the way of traffic. Sleet and slush soaked into her dress and her hair as she struggled to get to her feet. There were few pedestrians out in this weather, only a lady at the end of the street who stared in surprise.

SHE HAD MANAGED to jump out of the carriage onto her own street. As she was relatively unharmed, the goal must have been to ruin her. To frighten her.

And she was definitely unsettled. Disconcerted, even. More than a little frightened, to be truthful.

But she would not let that stop her.

Because she was also very, *very* angry. And an angry Spinster was something to behold. That fear they expected her to turn inward on herself would instead shoot from her like fiery arrows. And she intended to have very good aim.

If not at this exact moment, then eventually.

She needed to get herself to Spinster House first, but she could not go tearing off in this state. It would invite notice, questions, concerns. Gossip. She could not go home either, which was mere steps away. She would not do that to her parents. They would worry. More than was helpful. She could not blame them—she was quite sure she looked a fright. Already, someone stared at her from an open carriage window.

There was one immediate solution.
Close.
Convenient.
A terrible idea.

CHAPTER TWELVE

S YBIL KNOCKED ONCE at Montgomery House and was already slipping inside before the butler had finished opening the door. He was a frightfully proper sort, with whiskers that curled with the aid of pomade and a monocle he liked to look through with great disdain. But he was secretly fond of her, ever since she had shared her sugarplums one Christmas morning, reaching over the iron railing between their houses with her short, little arms.

"Good afternoon, Chevril," she greeted him with a weary smile, dropping onto the bench that was still sitting under a painting of a hunting dog no one in the family had ever owned. The bench was in the exact same place as it had been the one other time she had dared venture through the front door of dreary Montgomery House. It was that day she was fourteen and decided to bring a doll for the newly born Sophie and a basket of plums for Keir, who only stared at her. Rightfully so—who brought plums to a young man after his mother died? Especially when they had not spoken for months.

The things he had said to her then. In this very hall, by this very bench. That there were expectations of his title, that she was too much but also not enough. Beneath him. Still a child when he had grown up.

Words calculated to enrage her, now she thought about it.

She hated this hall, this bench.

Perhaps this was a bad idea.

He still stared at her, after all. Only now it was different. It was all different.

She nearly went up in flames, spent nights tangled and sweaty in the sheets, unable to stop replaying their trysts in her head, and he just went about his day, doing whatever it was that he did when he was not courting Lady Violetta and being pelted with snow.

She should come up with another plan. *Any* other plan.

But as she could not, and as she was desperate, she remained where she was.

If she was lucky, he would not be at home.

As she had not been lucky for a single moment since she woke up that morning, from spilling her breakfast tea on her dress to her abduction, she was not at all surprised when his footsteps sounded down the hall. The light struggled to get between the heavy drapes, the swaths of velvet.

There was, of course, just enough light to readily display the state of her hair: falling out of its pins in tangles.

The state of her face: flushed and blotchy. Red around her neck where the sack had been tied too tightly.

The state of her dress: wet and torn and wrinkled beyond what could be reasonably explained.

The state of her in general: bedraggled.

Chevril and Keir both stared at her. She tried a cheerful smile despite suddenly feeling bone tired and as if her veins were full of coffee and champagne bubbles and cold, sharp pins.

They continued to stare as a small puddle melted under her boots.

Keir was the first to speak. "What the hell happened to you?"

It was more of a roar. A bellow. From a man best known for his quiet, stoic commands.

"Good afternoon, Lord Blackburn," Sybil said, more primly than she had ever said anything in her entire life. "Chevril, might

I trouble you for a cup of tea?"

Chevril turned on his very well-kept heel and departed in what could only be called a canter. "And call for the doctor!" Keir called after him, his eyes never leaving her.

"I don't need a doctor," she assured him.

He did not look assured.

He finally crossed the marble floor and crouched in front of her. "Are you hurt?"

She shook her head. "Not a bit." All things considered. Although, truthfully, she felt several bruises blooming from her knee to her hip. She probably ought not mention those. "It was only a minor abduction."

Keir went still. As he had not been particularly restless, the effect was chilling. His eyes glittered. The fire popped somewhere in a room behind him, a warning. "I beg your pardon?"

"Miniscule," she insisted. She knew she should have kept her mouth shut. "Honestly, I'm not sure they knew what they were doing."

She felt certain they knew *exactly* what they were doing, but as Keir looked to be on the verge of some kind of apoplectic fit, she decided a small, comfortable lie was in order.

He stood slowly. "Are you telling me someone tried to *abduct* you?"

"Just a little?"

"*Who?*"

She looked up at him, looming and menacing, and felt inexplicably warm. Downright cheerful.

How odd.

"Who was it, Sybil? I want a fucking name."

"I don't know who it was," she said, blinking at his language. She was quite certain she had heard him curse more in the last five minutes than in the last five years. Not that they spent much time actually talking. Apparently, she had that effect on him. "They put a sack over my head."

She had thought he was a mountain before, but now he was

an avalanche, shivering on the precipice, ready to destroy entire villages, flatten anything in his way.

His jaw clenched and the tendons in his neck moved as he struggled to hold back a kind of primal storm she had not thought him capable of. And still, despite the icy fury in his eyes and the dangerous set of his mouth, he was indescribably gentle as he tugged her to her feet and brought her to the parlor, sitting her before the fire. He wrapped a blanket around her. Stared at her and added a second blanket. He had a third in his grasp when the housekeeper rolled in the tea cart.

"Thank you, Mrs. Hawkins," Sybil said. She glanced at Keir after he growled at her when she dared put a hand outside of her blanket cocoon. "I am beginning to feel like a sausage roll baking in a skillet."

"Just don't move for a full minute," he said, pouring her tea and bringing it to her even though he had a household of people hired to do just that. "A full minute where I know you are not racing horses in the snow or being grabbed off the damned street."

"I really am fine," she said before sipping her tea. It was too strong and too sweet. Perfect. How did he remember how she took her tea? She took a few more sips and waited until the set of his shoulders looked less like boulders ready to crack. He wasn't just an avalanche—he was an earthquake waiting to happen.

For her.

For any woman in her situation, no doubt, but at least a little bit for her.

She remembered this feeling.

If she grinned at him now, there was no telling what he would do.

Oh, it was tempting.

She set the cup down and wriggled free of the blankets. He scowled at her. "I'm sweltering," she protested.

"You're seeing the doctor when he gets here."

"I'm hot because you wrapped me up like a Christmas pudding on the boil, not because I am ill with a fever," she pointed out. "I went for an unexpected carriage ride, a couple of men blustered and brayed like donkeys, which is an insult to donkeys now that I think about it, because donkeys are charming. And now I'm fine. I only came here to clean up a bit so my parents would not worry. And because people were starting to stare." She froze. "Oh dear."

"What now? You were taken to Newgate Prison? Bedlam hospital? You saw a fairy king in Berkeley Square?"

She waved that away. "Of course not. It's only that if anyone saw me come here, it might make things awkward with Lady Violetta. Again. I didn't think. Again."

"I don't care about that."

He would, when he had a moment to think about it. "I'm so sorry. I promise I am not doing it on purpose."

He shook his head. "*That* gets more of a reaction from you than a kidnapping?" She shrugged. He scrubbed a hand down his face. "Sybil, you can't keep doing this."

"Doing what?"

"Whatever it is that gets you *abducted.*"

She shrugged again, even though it made the vein in his temple throb. "London is London."

"Most ladies live their entire lives in London without so much as a head cold. Never mind stealing horses and being abducted."

"*Barely* abducted."

"Sybil. You need a doctor. More tea. An evening of rest."

"Don't be silly," she said, kicking fully free of the blankets, lest he decide he could trap her inside them. "I have plans tonight."

"Cancel them."

"Certainly not."

"Then I'm going with you."

"To Miss Copperwhite's musicale?" she asked, very doubtfully.

He crossed his arms. "Yes."

She also crossed her arms. "You weren't invited."

"I am a marquess." It was confidence tipping into arrogance. But also, regrettably true. There were few doors closed to a marquess. Certainly not the drawing room doors of Miss Copperwhite's interminably long musicale on the south side of the river.

"It's going to be dreadfully dull."

Keir snorted. "Not if *you're* there."

"WHAT HAPPENED TO you?" Peony asked an hour later when Sybil managed to escape Keir's doctor and Mrs. Hawkins's bribery of fresh muffins with butter and jam and Chevril wringing his hands with worry. When she slipped out the door wearing one of Sophie's cloaks to hide her disarray, Keir was already waiting for her with his carriage.

He did not speak.

Not a single word when she gave him Priya's address, not a word when he tucked the warming brick under her boots, not even a word when she reminded him that Miss Copperwhite liked to sing an aria at her musicales. She believed she sang like an angel.

She did not.

Keir had insisted on walking her to the door, pausing only for his gaze to rake over her, leaving heat and a shivery kind of awareness. "I will be back at nine o'clock to pick you up."

"I already have an escort, thank you."

"Who?"

"Mrs. Farraway."

He'd frowned, confused. "Mrs. Farraway."

Mrs. Farraway was eighty-one years old and not known for her kindness.

"She needs a companion."

"Since when are you a companion? What aren't you telling me?"

"Oh, a great deal, I imagine."

He'd nearly smiled. She knew the signs now. The twitch at the corner of his mouth, the way he tightened his lips as though to smile at her was dangerous. It might well be—only for her, surely not for him. He was immune to her smiles. If not her particular kind of pandemonium.

No one was immune to it, which was rather the point.

Even when it was uncomfortable to be judged and whispered about. It would happen regardless, so she may as well make use of it. They were not idle words she had spoken to Sophie about using her own reputation as a weapon that cut away instead of toward oneself.

Keir had only turned and stridden off without a backward glance.

And now she was in the Fern Parlor while the other Spinsters stared at her.

"Was that Lord Blackburn?" Priya asked from her chair, which was nowhere near a window or even the front of the house. Her ability to know things really was disconcerting.

"Yes."

"Interesting," Matilda said, raising her brows.

"It is the least interesting thing that happened to me today, actually." And yet it wasn't. And it was far more enjoyable to think about him than it was to focus on her bruises and her aching knee and shoulder.

"Well, someone pushed me onto Piccadilly Road last night," Matilda said. "I could have been flattened. May the crows eat their eyeballs."

Sybil tilted her head. "Really?"

"I'm fine."

"I'm fine too."

"Why, what happened to you?"

"I was abducted not two hours ago."

Peony sat up straighter. "Did you break all their teeth?"

"Alas, no. And that *is* vexing."

"Someone dropped a heavy box from a window right above

my head," Emmeline added.

Matilda stared at her. "You never told me that!"

"You were on a rampage about Piccadilly traffic."

"I can rampage for the both of us!"

"Yes, I know, darling."

"Three accidents," Priya said. "How… coincidental."

"You don't believe in coincidence," Sybil reminded her.

"No, I do not."

The women exchanged grim glances. The fury boiling beneath the surface was the kind that burned cities to ash.

"It's clear someone has figured out at least three members of the Spinster Society."

"And they do not like us very much," Sybil said. "Which is quite discourteous, really. We are *delightful*."

"Peony?" Priya asked. "What about you?"

"I am also delightful, but I did not go out last night."

"And no one came here?

Peony shook her head.

"Good."

"Kitty had something to add about the symbol. As did my abductors," Sybil said, reaching for the tea. If her hand trembled faintly, no one mentioned it. "It was suggested to her that it is the mark of a society of gentlemen."

"Is it indeed." Priya's eyes narrowed.

"And in the carriage, one of the fellows, who goes by the name of Alfie, said something about Minos."

"Minos was the king of Knossos in ancient Crete. When his son was killed in Athens, he forced them to send seven girls and seven boys every nine years to enter the labyrinth."

"The same labyrinth with the minotaur. The man with a bull's head?" Emmeline asked.

"The very same. They were eaten."

"What a lovely nom de guerre. Very subtle."

"But is it a person or a society?" Priya asked. "Did Alfie say anything to help us there?"

"Either? Both? I can't be sure. The suggestion is that he or they are not to be trifled with."

Peony smiled, showing all of her teeth. "I happen to like trifle."

"It's not much to go on," Sybil admitted. "But thank you, Alfie, you incompetent ass."

"We shall find him, I can assure you of that."

"What do we do in the meantime?" Emmeline asked.

"For one thing, we tell our wife when someone tries to crush our skull," Matilda muttered, her Spanish accent thickening. She spoke at least seven languages but always reverted to her mother tongue when upset.

"We carry on as best we can," Priya added. "Although it is definitely not safe anymore." A line formed between her brows.

"It's never been perfectly safe," Sybil pointed out with a shrug. She had the scars to prove it. And did not regret a single one. "And if all of us miraculously survived assorted attempts, it seems likely this *was* just a warning, which they said as much to me. An order to stop." She lifted her chin. "And I do not take orders."

"And I know just where they can stuff those orders," Peony muttered.

"That's what I said! They were not keen on hearing my suggestion. There were two men, maybe three. No aristocratic accents, though I suppose they could have been using street cant to throw me off. Seems unlikely. More likely they were hired off the street so as not to be accidentally recognized. It was broad daylight, after all. Very risky."

"Yes, I do not care for that either," Priya said, gold bangles flashing as she drummed her fingers on the armrest of her chair. "Too bold by half."

"It was a hackney carriage. I could not see inside, given as there was a sack over my head."

"Very rude indeed," Matilda said.

"Quite. But if someone is coming for us," Sybil added, "then I intend to do as much damage as I can in the meantime. Especially as we appear to be effective in meddling in 'men's affairs'."

"I am going to have that printed on my calling cards," Emmeline murmured. *"Meddling in Men's Affairs Since 1815."*

"I think I'll open a second house," Priya said. Sybil could all but see the cogs and wheels turning inside her head. "Just in case. Clearly, we are no longer as secure—or as secret—as we once were. If they are coming for us one by one, then they already know too much."

"And use this house for misdirection?" Sybil asked.

"Precisely."

"Well, I'm staying here," Peony declared. Everyone knew she would not leave the heated pool or her obstacle course for love or money. Or threat to life and limb, as it were.

"As are we," Emmeline added, her fingers linking with Matilda's. "This is our home."

They looked at Sybil. She snorted. "What do you think? But first, I must change for the Copperwhite musicale."

"You were already abducted today." Matilda winced in sympathy. "Haven't you suffered enough?"

"Sadly, no. I'm to be Mrs. Farraway's companion."

"Worse and worse."

"Care to take my place?"

"I'd rather be pushed into traffic again."

CHAPTER THIRTEEN

MRS. COPPERWHITE'S MUSICALE was worse than Sybil could have predicted.

So much worse.

Mrs. Farraway was a cantankerous old woman who enjoyed having people do her bidding. She was snobbish and often cruel.

But also useful.

Because she was Mrs. Copperwhite's godmother and therefore invited to every musicale. And as Miss Copperwhite was in possession of a number of love letters written to her brother from a Lady Venetia, Sybil also needed to be in attendance. Lady Venetia, who did not wish to be ruined or married to a man who sought to blackmail her into a wedding. And yet she was the one Society would brand unreasonable and solely culpable. As if she was the only one writing racy, scandalous letters. As if Mr. Copperwhite had not replied in kind.

She had dismal taste, clearly, but that hardly demanded a lifetime of penance to a man such as him. He had ignored her for two years, and now that she had come into an inheritance, he'd popped back up, all oily flattery and not-so-subtle threats.

He was clever enough not to keep the letters at his home, which Emmeline had already searched.

He was not, however, clever enough not to brag about it.

And so, Sybil's current mission was to bow her head meekly

as the companion Miss Grey while following dozens of unnecessary orders given solely to remind her of her place. That was the real reason Mrs. Farraway hired a companion.

Sybil fetched her shawl from the front hall, then her smelling salts from her reticule, then returned the shawl because it was far too warm by the fire and she ought to have known better. She fetched a glass of wine, a plate of cheese with dates and figs. She moved Mrs. Farraway's chair away from the fire to the window and then back again, being scolded for scratching the floor. "Miss Grey, do stop woolgathering. I asked you to set up my chair in the conservatory for the performance."

She hadn't asked for any such thing.

But as the conservatory was in another part of the house and that served Sybil's true purpose, she nodded meekly. "Yes, Mrs. Farraway."

Another lady smirked, enjoying the show. There was nothing a gathering such as this loved as much as someone being taken down a peg. Several pegs. Surely there were no pegs left.

And then the whispering abruptly changed tone and cadence. It lightened, like a dozen songbirds had suddenly congregated in the parlor. Sybil turned, frowning, toward the new guest.

Keir Montgomery, Marquess Blackburn.

He bowed to the room at large, finding her immediately. His green eyes were steady and clear. Sybil did not alter her frown, even though people did not frown at a marquess, especially not companions like Miss Grey. He had threatened to follow her here, but she had not believed him. No one came to this musicale without very good reason. She had a very good reason. Keir did not.

He would remember that when his ears began to bleed.

"My chair, Miss Grey," Mrs. Farraway snapped. "At once."

Keir was the one frowning now. She shot him a quelling glance. If he ruined her cover, she would murder him, plain and simple. No one knew Lady Sybil in this part of London.

"Of course, Mrs. Farraway."

Sybil expected Keir's frown to drop away entirely at her docility. He would be beside himself with the evidence that she *could*, in fact, be demure. That she could curtsy with her head bent modestly. That she could be no trouble at all.

Instead, his eyes narrowed.

Rather alarmingly.

Sybil turned on her heel and darted away.

MISS COPPERWHITE WAS more clever than expected.

And it was annoying.

Sybil made sure Mrs. Farraway's chair had two cushions, a shawl against the chill from the windows, was near the candles but not *too* near the candles, and next to a table set with a goblet of sherry and a silver bowl of hard candies. Then she hurried up the stairs, keeping clear of the household staff. A pause behind a potted tree, a moment to flatten herself behind a cabinet carved with lilies, and then she was inside Miss Copperwhite's bedchamber.

Everything was frothed with lace, from the curtains to the coverlet. The ceiling was painted like the sky over a Roman villa, feathery olive branches, doves, Corinthian marble columns. There was a writing desk under a window, a chamber pot behind a screen. A hundred usual hiding spots for heirlooms or private journals or coins.

None of those places hid a packet of explicit love letters.

"Blast," Sybil muttered, crawling half under the bed in case they had been stuffed under the mattress. They had not.

And she could not be away from the guests any longer. It might rouse suspicion. She would have to try another room, perhaps while Miss Copperwhite was singing.

"There you are," Mrs. Farraway snapped as soon as Sybil returned. The guests were rising to move to the conservatory. Slowly and somewhat reluctantly, it had to be said. "What use are you to me if you go galivanting off?"

"My apologies."

"Well, don't stand about. Help me up."

Sybil helped her to her feet and handed Mrs. Farraway her cane. The long strand of jet beads Mrs. Farraway wore around her neck swung as she walked, catching the light.

"Don't dawdle."

"Yes, Mrs. Farraway."

IN THE HALL, Keir stepped up beside her.

"What are you doing here?" she asked out of the side of her mouth.

"*You* are here," he replied as though that was reason enough. "*Miss Grey.*"

"That does not answer my question," she pointed out, because it could not be reason enough.

"Need I remind you that you were abducted today?" he said, exasperated. "Apparently, I do."

"That was hours ago."

"I do not like the way that woman speaks to you. Let me take you home."

Warmth suffused her, spilling behind her ribcage, filling her up. It was a lovely thing for him to say, for some reason made lovelier by his disgruntled, grumbling tone. "I can't go until I find what I came for."

"Which is?"

"None of your business." Sybil grinned at him. "My lord."

"How did I know you were going to say that?"

"Damn, I do hate to be predictable."

"No need to concern yourself with that, I assure you."

"Miss Grey, do not make eyes at Lord Blackburn," Mrs. Farraway scolded, purely with the intent to embarrass her. One of the other ladies snickered. "It is not seemly in one of your standing."

"We do not kick old ladies," Sybil muttered under her breath. "We do not kick old ladies."

"*I'll* kick her if you like," Keir muttered back drily.

She wanted to grin at him again.

She wanted to do a lot of things.

Instead, she lowered her chin and tried not to look like she wanted to punch half a dozen of the guests as well as kick an old lady. "You can do something for me," she whispered.

"Anything."

Oh. Well, that was lovely too.

"Keep their attention."

He sighed. "You owe me, Miss Grey."

"You came here unbidden. I did try to warn you."

"So you did." The corner of his mouth twitched. "But dear God, woman. This is worse than Almack's Assembly."

"Poor Keir," she cooed. "Single marquesses with all their teeth do not grow on trees, you know."

He shot her a look that inexplicably made her tingle down to her toes. It made her cheeks flush, and she did not know why, as it was stern, exasperated, begrudgingly fond. It was hardly scandalous.

And yet.

It did things to her insides. To her blood and her thighs. To her nipples, suddenly tightening under her stays.

She swallowed, hoping he did not notice her reaction. She wove around the outskirts of the gathered guests finding their seats as he strode forward, tall and handsome and entirely too big for the overly fussy chairs.

"Ladies, allow me to assist you." His rough-soft voice galvanized everyone near him. Several toes were trod upon, then deliberately crushed under heels as the battle to sit next to him commenced. He shot Sybil one more look, commiserating but also promising punishment.

Distracting.

Very distracting.

"Cover your hair, girl. It's far too bright. Did you use lemons? Vain thing," Mrs. Farraway muttered, fussing with her shawl. It was fringed with glass beads. She did hate to look frail enough to need a blanket, even in winter.

Sybil was only glad that the dye she had used in her hair was finally washing away.

"So brassy," someone sniffed.

"Well, blood will tell."

Keir turned his head very slowly at that last comment. His jaw tightened.

"Sit back there and don't be a nuisance," Mrs. Farraway ordered Sybil. "Better yet, go down to the kitchen and make sure they have the right spices for my mulled wine."

"Of course, Mrs. Farraway."

"Lord Blackburn," a woman chirped. "Are you growling?"

"Certainly not. The chair creaked." When Sybil widened her eyes at him, he sighed. "Miss Leonard, there is a spare seat here next to me."

A marquess inviting a merchant's daughter to join him at a public gathering was unheard of. It captured everyone's attention. They would gossip about him until Christmas. Sybil was impressed. Keir had a future in subterfuge. Who would have guessed?

She hurried out, avoiding the singing if not the derision. She'd rather avoid the singing, to be quite honest. More than one guest had already surreptitiously slipped balls of soft beeswax into their ears to muffle the sound.

There was snow at the windows, hot tea and pastries with raspberry preserves. Comfortable cushions. Sybil still vastly preferred her exile to the stuffy kitchen, and then back upstairs to Miss Copperwhite's morning room.

Perhaps it was not that she was so very clever, only that she was as unworried as her brother, with no thought that anyone might get the best of them.

The morning room was pretty and tidy, decorated in shades of cheerful yellow and a great many paintings of tulips. There were decorative boxes for ribbons, pens, a penknife inlaid with pearl. And a basket of needlepoint.

And at the bottom of the basket: a packet of letters tied with a blue ribbon.

Once Sybil had confirmed they were indeed the letters written by Miss Venetia, she slipped them inside one of the many pockets tied around her waist. She might not be wearing her cloak-of-many-pockets, but a Spinster was always prepared.

Which meant that she was also wearing a sturdy pair of boots, which helped enormously once the musicale was finished and Mrs. Farraway left in her carriage without a word to Sybil, leaving her to walk home in the snow. As expected. Mrs. Farraway was nothing if not predictable. She did not actually require a companion out of Sybil, only someone to torture every now and again to cement her place in the world.

Sybil was not the least bit surprised to find Keir's carriage waiting at the road. He leaned against it, snow gathering in his dark hair, arms crossed as though he was perfectly comfortable to wait the rest of the night. "Get in, Miss Grey."

"I'm not going home."

"I'll take you anywhere you want to go."

CHAPTER FOURTEEN

KEIR'S COACHMAN TOOK them to Spinster House. The bridge was all sleet and frozen mud as they crossed the river to the north side. It would have been dismal to cross on foot, even if the falling snow *was* pretty. The cold would have easily gripped her, set her ankle to aching, her mind to running in jagged circles.

Instead, she was back inside a warm carriage with Keir as if it was a perfectly normal thing for him to see her home from horse races and secret missions during musicales.

"Thank you," Sybil said, her feet perched on the wrapped warming brick. She still liked the cold sneaking in through the sides of the door, pinkening her cheeks. But she no longer cared for it to touch the rest of her for too long. She was going to have to work on that.

But not tonight.

Tonight, she was comfortable and pleased with her success and sitting across from a ruggedly beautiful man who, although too serious for his own good, had helped her at some cost to his dignity.

And dignity was everything to a Montgomery.

They might not know Minos's true identity, or how he knew so much about them, or even why he was coming after them. They could guess that they had foiled one of his plans, but it was just a guess.

But they *could* help Miss Venetia. And Miss Maddox. And any number of other ladies in the meantime. And it was all the sweeter now that each victory was a thumbing of their noses at their unknown attacker. It was worth every insult, every disdainful sniff, every loud mutter about her lineage, or lack thereof.

Although Keir, it seemed, did not agree.

"Don't ask me to sit by again while they treat you like that," he said. "I would have an easier time carrying a house on my back. And the way you bowed your head meekly..." He shuddered. "Look at me, I'm sweating."

She had to smile as the carriage pulled to a stop. He was adorable. Somehow, stern, solemn, inscrutable Keir Montgomery was also adorable.

That didn't seem fair.

"I didn't think marquesses were allowed to sweat. I'm sure it's a rule."

"Clearly, a rule made by someone who has never met *you*."

She bit her tongue on a highly inappropriate suggestion about other ways to make him sweat. He was not for her and she was not for him.

It was getting harder and harder to remember that.

Spinster House waited, with lamplight at the windows, welcoming in the swirls of snow. One of the footmen had already shoveled the walk. It would smell like flowers and fire and warm, delicious things cooking in the oven. It was home.

And yet she wanted to linger in the carriage, which was not quite large enough to fit Keir, with melting snow dripping from her cloak and hair. His eyes were on her. She licked her lower lip and his gaze flared. An answering tingle sparked low in her belly.

"I'll walk you to your door," he finally said.

SOME THINGS WERE simple enough.

She enjoyed Keir's company and did not wish for him to say goodnight just yet.

If it was torture of a kind, she was only torturing herself.

"Would you like some tea? And shortbread? We have a cook who makes shortbread like your Scottish granny."

He smiled briefly. "My Scottish granny did not make short-bread."

"Oh."

"But surely, had she done so, it would have far surpassed anything made by your English cook."

"Is that a challenge?"

"Absolutely."

She was grinning as she led him inside the house. He frowned at the empty hall, the oil lamp burning on a marble-topped table with carved peacocks. "Where's your butler?"

"We keep odd hours," Sybil explained, untying the knot of her cape ribbons. "There's no sense in keeping everyone up all night just to open a door for us. I'm perfectly capable of moving my arms. I've been doing so for nearly thirty years." She was supposed to hide her age, to be demure about her spinsterhood.

Not in this house.

"There *is* sense in it when someone just tried to abduct you," Keir grumbled.

"We have sturdy locks." She took his hat and his gloves and tossed them carelessly onto a chair. "And footmen."

"Footmen."

"Aye," one of the footmen said, appearing at the end of the hall. "All right, miss?"

"Yes, thank you, Peter."

"Peter, is it?" Keir asked, peering down the hall. Sybil saw the exact moment he noticed the other man's military bearing, the knife at his boot. He nodded. "Good man."

Sybil took Keir to the parlor because it seemed a bit brave to drag him to her bedchamber and beg him to undress her. With his teeth. Or to let her undress him. With her teeth. Not that they had never done so, just not like this. Not without a clear escape route.

Keir followed her, no doubt perfectly aware of the fact that this was scandalous enough for a man like him. A deserted parlor with a fire burning low and snow at the window was precisely a place where a lady was seduced by a scoundrel. If she was lucky.

"And I'm not the scoundrel here," he said. "That distinction belongs entirely to you."

He was not precisely wrong, she supposed.

How delightful.

Sybil tried to get her wayward thoughts under control as she had not even realized she had spoken out loud "Just so you know, our cook is French."

"I should have guessed."

"And I shouldn't like to bother her for tea at this hour."

"Lured by the promise of tea and shortbread and left wanting." He shook his head, as if disappointed. "Worse and worse."

"I do have shortbread, though." Sybil went to the side table, always well stocked with whisky and brandy and chocolate fondants. Also: knives, sharpened hatpins, bundles of herbs with various unsavory uses. Hopefully, Keir would not notice those. "And whisky."

"Sybil?"

"Yes?"

"May I tell you a secret?"

She turned to stare at him. "*You* have secrets?"

That fond twitch of his mouth again. "Everyone has secrets, Sybil."

As he was standing in a house filled to the rafters with secrets, she did not disagree. "And yours is?"

He bent his head closer, eyes shining, tone heavy with the gravity of what he was about to impart. She held her breath because he was so close and she liked it so much. And he never told her secrets anymore. "I do not care for whisky," he said.

She gasped on a chuckle. "Blasphemy."

He nodded gravely. "Don't tell my Scottish granny. Now, *she* loved whisky."

Sybil shook her head, clicking her tongue. "You've given me a dangerous power over you, Keir Montgomery. Was that wise, do you think?"

"You already have power over me," he said, but he murmured it so softly that she was half convinced she had misheard him.

Pity.

She cleared her throat. "Brandy, instead?"

"Please."

Now that she had him here in the parlor, she could not think of a single thing to do with him that was not deeply scandalous. Salacious, even.

He swallowed his liqueur, and she watched the muscles of his strong throat working above his simple cravat and wondered if she was going mad. Neck muscles were not sensual. Were they? Why was she mesmerized?

"Don't look at me like that, Sybil," Keir said quietly, roughly.

She swallowed, caught. "Why not? I mean to say, what do you mean?"

He put his brandy down carefully, as though everything was made of glass, not just the cup. As if he might break apart.

As if he might like to look at her the way she was looking at him.

"I think you know."

"I don't think I do."

"Dangerous games, my little scoundrel."

"And you play it safe."

"Yes. But there's nothing safe about you, is there, Sybil?" The way he said her name made her toes curl, as did the way he advanced toward her, crossing the carpet in two giant strides. She had to tip her head back to meet his gaze.

They stood there for a long moment, the fire crackling, the hot, sweet taste of brandy on her tongue, the warmth of his body just barely touching hers. His mouth so close, so close.

Closer still.

And then, because they were in a house full of women who meddled in the affairs of men, it was at that very moment that a stone crashed through the window, shattering the glass.

CHAPTER FIFTEEN

KEIR HEARD THE crack and something inside him cracked as well. His entire body reacted, already on painful alert since Sybil had casually strolled into his house and declared she had been taken off the damned street. And now even more on alert standing so close to him in the soft shadows as her lips parted on what he hoped was simply the word "yes."

Instead: a rock, a broken window, a shot of cold fear down his spine.

At least, thank God, he was close enough to seize her up in his arms, if not exactly in the way he would have preferred. As he didn't know immediately that it was a rock and not a musket ball or a gunpowder bomb, he had her tucked under his body before his brain could fully process what was happening.

She squeaked. He glanced down, making certain that every part of her was shielded by his body. He had the foresight to cradle her head when he tossed her down onto the floor. He was abruptly aware that gentlemen did not toss ladies onto the floor, no matter the plush quality of the hand-knotted carpets. Sybil blinked up at him, a flush on her cheeks, her breath startled from her lungs. Unharmed. *Thank God.*

He let out his own breath, every muscle still tense. "Are you hurt?"

"Not a bit," she assured him. "Are *you* hurt?"

"No."

"Are you sure?"

"Yes."

"Your face is funny."

"Thanks very much." He frowned. "I don't know what to say to that." That thought was a constant companion when they were together, and he found he did not mind it. He had missed it, in fact.

The attacks on her person, he minded very much.

"Goodness," she said. "That lady earlier was quite right. You do growl."

He eased off her purely to assess any remaining danger and because he did not wish to crush her. Not because he wished to be anywhere else, because he most certainly did not. His heart thundered in his chest as he helped her to her feet, tucking her behind him, where she, naturally, did not remain. "Sybil, stay behind me."

He growled it, of course.

"Someone threw a rock through our window!" She didn't weep or flutter. Not his Sybil. Instead, she swore like a sailor. A drunk sailor on leave. A pirate. He knew several men who considered themselves worldly and debauched who would have blushed. He might have also if he wasn't occupied with making sure she was safe.

Nothing else was acceptable.

He was peering out the window as the footman burst through the door. Keir was gratified to see him wielding that dagger. "Bastard took off through the garden and over the fence into the park," Keir said. "I can see his bloody footprints."

The footman nodded. "I'll follow."

Keir would have dearly loved to join him, if only to tear that miscreant limb from limb. But the thought of leaving Sybil alone made him physically ill.

"I doubt he'll find anyone," Sybil muttered, bending to pick up the rock. "The very reason we are on the edge of the Park is because it affords so much space and privacy."

Keir batted her hand away. "Give me that."

"It's just a rock."

"So you say. But I don't know of many drawing rooms that have rocks thrown through their windows."

"You do not know terribly interesting people, then."

"I think you might be right about that," he said, examining the rock, which was just that: a rock. There was, however, a note tied round it with string.

Sybil peered around his shoulder to read it. *"You were warned."* She scoffed. "That's rather uninspired."

Keir wrestled the waves of fury building inside his ribcage. "Who would do this?"

Sybil shrugged. "Who knows?" she asked, airily. So airily it set his teeth on edge.

"Sybil Taunton."

"Keir Montgomery."

He was growling again. "Explain."

"Oh, I thought we were just saying each other's names."

The urge to toss her over his shoulder and take her away was very nearly overwhelming. He exhaled through his nose. Someone had once told him it was calming. That someone was used to dealing with the aftereffects of war and street riots. Not Miss Sybil Taunton.

A little deep breathing was not enough. Not nearly enough.

"Sybil, what is this house, really?"

"Just a house."

"Try again."

"It's a… finishing school."

"Sybil." He pinched the bridge of his nose.

"Yes?"

"Exactly how daft do you think I am?" She opened her mouth to reply, then snapped it shut when he tilted his head. "Careful."

She sniffed. "Well, you did ask."

"My mistake."

"Just so long as we are clear on that point."

He had never wanted to spank someone and kiss them sense-less at the same time. Strangling was also not out of the question. "Are you going to tell me the truth?"

"I don't know," she admitted.

He sighed. "Well, I suppose that's something."

"That's it?" She looked up at him suspiciously. The firelight glimmered in her hair. And over the plain dress he wanted to strip from her body. She ought to wear only the very best silks, muslins, velvets. Or better yet, nothing at all.

"If we've established that I am not so daft as to believe this is a finishing school, then let us also assume that I am not so daft as to think Sybil Taunton can be forced into anything."

"What a lovely thing to say," she beamed.

"I think *you* might be the daft one."

"That's less lovely of you." She shrugged one shoulder. "But also very likely."

The footman returned with snow in his hair and a disgruntled expression, and a second footman carrying a plank of wood. "No luck," he said. "Footprints got lost in the mess out there."

"As expected," Sybil said. "It's not your fault."

"I'll send word to Mr. Gallagher."

"It can wait until morning."

"With respect, Miss Taunton, he would string me from the nearest lamppost by my insides."

"Fair enough."

The second footman had already begun nailing the plank over the broken window. Sybil shivered at the cold wind finding its way inside. Keir had not noticed right away—he was boiling with anger and the sudden desire to burn down London. Cursing himself, he herded her away from the window. "Come on, then."

"What? Where?"

"You're cold." He nudged her up the stairs, noting the paint-ings on the wall, mostly of women, like Judith slaying Holofernes, or the Furies, also holding the decapitated heads of men who had wronged them. Joan of Arc watched them from the landing, her eyes glowing and otherworldly. "Where's your chamber?"

"Not that one—that belongs to Matilda and Emmeline. I'm just here on the left."

He marched inside, added coal to the grate, made sure the fire was burning, and then marched back out again, very carefully not looking toward the bed where he was desperate to imagine Sybil sprawled out wearing nothing but her stockings. To actually have the luxury of time when he got his hands on her.

He snagged one of her chairs and set it down in the hall. It was drafty and shadowy and would still afford him a far better night's rest than his own feather bed and roaring fire too many streets away. Sybil just stared at him, still standing in the doorway. "What are you doing?" she asked.

"I'm getting comfortable." He sat back in the chair, praying it wouldn't snap under him.

"You don't have to stay, you know," she pointed out. "I'm perfectly safe here."

He opened one eye, calm. Deeply incredulous. "Do you really think I'm going to leave you alone?"

"But…"

"Out of the question, Sybil."

"There are several armed footmen just downstairs."

"Not good enough."

She watched him for a moment, nibbling on her lower lip in a way that made him hard enough to wonder if he was doing himself an injury. If he would make it through the night.

"You could… come inside," she suggested softly. "I know we don't usually…"

He took too long to answer because he wasn't entirely sure she had actually spoken or if he had conjured it up out of sheer desperation and want.

"Unless"—she flushed, clearly embarrassed—"you don't want me," she added in a mildly horrified whisper. "Not really. Not like this."

He only stared at her.

"It's fine," she rushed on, forcing a smile. "It's only when we can't help ourselves. Extenuating circumstances, as you said. Perfectly understandable. I'm not... That is. It's fine!" Her smile was too wide, too bright.

"Extenuating circumstances?" he echoed because clearly he had lost his hearing or else she had lost her mind.

"You don't owe me an explanation." She gripped the door, preparing to shut it in his face. Plotting her escape.

When he grabbed the door, she struggled against his grip but it did not budge. Not one centimeter. The idea of not wanting her was so absurd that he could only glower at her while he fought every instinct that begged to prove her wrong. Very, very wrong. His voice was low and rough and felt ripped from him when he demanded: "You think I don't want you?"

She swallowed.

"Sybil," he stated calmly, "I have wanted you for days, months. Bloody *years*. All I do is want you, with every single breath. It is the thing I was put on this earth to do. Why do you think that every time I swear to stay away from you, I fail?"

Her lips parted, torturing him.

He stepped closer, crowding her until her bottom hit an ornamental table. He kicked the door shut behind him, not taking his eyes from her. Her intake of breath shuddered, soft, tempting. He wanted to drink it from her mouth. He did not usually allow himself the indulgence of staring at her.

"You think I don't want you?" He laughed, but there was no humor in it. It was a promise. Almost dangerous. "You have no idea the things I want to do to you. Even now. Even after all the times we have found each other in secret."

He was so close now and still not close enough, his mouth barely touching her cheek as he whispered into her ear. The smell of her soap and her warm skin tickling his nostrils. Her breasts brushing against his chest as she breathed, but otherwise still as a deer in the woods. It was the most delicious kind of torture. They were usually already burning up by now.

"I want to put my mouth to every part of your body, each and every single night like a prayer. I want to take you against this wall. In a bed, on a chair. In the goddamned carriage. I want you naked for days. For *weeks*. So I can finally, *finally*, take my goddamn time."

Her eyes were wide, her cheeks pink. He took one step back, another. His chest felt too tight now that his body was too far from hers. Would she tell him to leave? Call one of her footmen? This was beyond impropriety. This was not being overcome. This was *choosing*.

No more games. No more hiding.

Her smile was no longer bright and forced. It was instead the very epitome of temptation. Her voice, stunned and curious and so damned sultry, might actually kill him on the spot.

"Then why aren't you touching me already?" she whispered.

He swore. Commanded his body to stay where it was. His cock pressed against the placket of his pants. "Because this has to be your decision. Eyes open." He curled his hands into fists so he would not reach for her. It would be different this time. They would have words. Promises. Everything. "Say yes, Sybil," he murmured. "God, please say yes."

She tilted her chin up. "Keir?"

"Yes?"

"Yes."

And then she launched herself at him.

CHAPTER SIXTEEN

SYBIL WAS NOT entirely sure that she was not imagining Keir's beautifully filthy words—at least until she wrapped her arms around his neck and her legs around his hips. He barely shifted, catching her easily. His glass-green eyes were swallowed by dark pupils, watching her with a kind of stunned and vicious joy. She was so desperate for him, swollen and throbbing, that she might find her release just by shifting her position slightly against his hardness. She could lose herself, right here and right now.

Instead, she eased back slightly but did not let go.

Eyes open.

"What about Lady Violetta?" Sybil asked quietly. She didn't *want* to ask. She wanted to pretend that his answer did not matter. That nothing mattered but this moment. Nothing but the thread between them tightening, tightening. But that was not the way the world worked. She already knew it was not the way he worked, despite evidence to the contrary.

"What of her?"

"You're courting her," she reminded him even as she wished she could just keep her mouth shut for once in her blessed life. "I am sure she would not care for this, even if you are not officially betrothed." She had always known they would end.

"We are not betrothed," he said. She nodded. She did not know what else to do. She wanted that to be enough. "And I am not courting her."

"I underst—" Sybil broke off. "I'm sorry, did you…?"

She must have heard him wrong. She was not prone to hallucinations, but she supposed anyone might succumb when wrapped around a burly Scotsman who looked as if it was taking every ounce of his strength not to devour her.

"I spoke to Lady Violetta after the horse race."

"You… did?"

"Yes. It seemed the only decent thing to do."

And so it was. For him. Her very dutiful and honorable marquess to the core. That was why his sudden cut direct by the front door of his house and the ensuing silence at the garden fence had hurt so much all of those years ago. Because he always strove to do what was right. And she was wrong for him, for what he wanted from his life. But tonight, she refused to let any of that matter.

"I cannot possibly court another woman when I cannot keep my hands off you. I was a fool to think I could."

"Was she very upset?"

"No," he replied drily. "She was not the least bit fazed. Her mother, however, howled."

"I am sure she did."

"Loudly. It startled the cat."

She would have this night.

And then she would carry on.

Sybil knew how to carry on.

"Let me love you, Sybil," he said roughly. "There's no one to stop us now."

There was all of Society and all of his very beloved rules to stop them.

But again, not tonight.

Not tonight.

When she kissed him, it was slow and deep. Heat swelled, as it always did, but they struggled to stretch the moment. Not to hurry because someone might find them, but because they might start thinking clearly again. He cradled her bottom, pulling her legs wider around him, dragging her center over his hardness, again and again. Teasing her, tormenting her, whetting her appetite for him until she made soft, mewling noises in her throat. He chased them with his mouth and his teeth, dragging sucking kisses along her neck. She shivered in his arms, digging her fingers into his hair.

He crossed the room in two great strides, and the muscles of his shoulders worked under her fingertips. She wanted to see them, wanted to run her tongue along his skin. Wanted to bite them. She plucked at his cravat as he set her down on the edge of the bed, chuckling even as he continued to kiss her. He sounded *happy*. Not tortured.

She threw the cravat on the floor and watched as he made quick work of his waistcoat and tugged his lawn shirt over his head. The firelight played over the soft pelt of hair, the thickness of his torso, all ridges and strength and padding of warm flesh over muscle. His dark hair was tousled from her hands; his green eyes gleamed like sea glass.

She didn't know where to look because she wanted to see everything all at once. She had never really had the opportunity before. They had not allowed it of themselves. Of each other.

He raised an eyebrow. He knew her too well.

She narrowed her eyes in response.

And then he dropped to his knees in front of her and she nearly lost the ability to speak. Everything that was not Keir faded into the background: the crackling fire, the cold draft at the window, the messy counterpane behind her because she had forgotten to make her bed again. There was only Keir, his mouth, the expanse of his burly chest, his hands fisting in the hem of her skirts. "Eyes on me," he demanded.

He didn't shove her skirts up abruptly, not this time. He was methodical, precise, as he pushed them up to her knees, dragging his fingers back down along the inside of her calves. He pulled at the laces of her shoes and put them aside. Next, he reached for her stockings, catching and keeping her gaze as he rolled one down and then the other. She wished she was wearing a prettier gown, silkier stockings.

His palm brushed her ankle and she winced.

He froze. "Did I hurt you?"

She shook her head, biting her lower lip. No need to get all missish and silly over a few scars. He must have noticed them before, even if he had not said anything. Then again, everything they did was usually furtive and tucked into the shadows. She had not removed her stockings the night of the fireworks. There was no time. "I… have some scars," she said. "You needn't look."

His fingers tightened around her, as if she had threatened to bolt. "Does it hurt?"

"No."

"Do you promise?"

"Yes, of course." She forced a smile, feeling foolish. "It's nothing."

He waited a moment, another. His jaw clenched. "I know about Eastbourne."

She stared at him. "You do? How?"

"I just do. May he rot."

"Oh." He rubbed her ankles, up her legs, and it was nice. More than nice. Some of the tension released from her, and she could concentrate on the much more pleasurable warmth tingling through her from his touch. "You look angry."

"I *am* angry."

"Someone burned down his cellar," she said. She was glad for it. It helped a little, even if it shouldn't.

"I know," Keir said. "It was me."

Sybil blinked at him. He had never taken her quite as much by surprise as he did with that statement. And that was including that day by the front door. The time he had climbed a tree to rescue her cat. "But that was before…"

"Before?"

"Before." She made a helpless motion with her hand meant to

encompass everything that was between them. Everything that wasn't. "This."

"Was it?" He sounded so calm. So unlike a man who had burned down a cellar. "Sybil, I've known you for a long time, and there has only ever been this. No before, and certainly no *after*."

"So you burned down his cellar?"

"I would have burned down his house too, but there were servants inside."

She giggled—she couldn't help it. It was so… unexpected. Lovely in its own way. And mad. Definitely mad. "That does not sound like the actions of the Marquess of Most Righteous Order and Decorum."

"It was justice, plain and simple. And I know Parliament— they might have taken too long to act, if at all." He nudged closer, widening her knees. "How many lordly titles do you plan on giving me?"

"As many as I can think up."

"You only make them up when you think I am being pompous and stodgy."

She grinned. "Yes."

"Then I hope you have a good imagination," he added drily.

Her grin widened. "Are you saying I'm right?"

"Is that what you want to hear?"

She fluttered her eyelashes. "Yes, please."

"Then yes, you are, on occasion, right. Now, do you mind very much?" he added sternly. "I am in the middle of something, if you please."

"By all means, your lordship."

He pressed closer still, and the heat in her center liquefied. He tugged up her outer skirts, pushing them around her waist. Then her petticoats, tucking them carefully. His sides, warm and bare, tickled her inner thighs. It was nice to not have to rush.

But he was taking too long.

"Keir," she said, reaching for her gown to help him. All of her dresses were constructed so she did not require a lady's maid, and even her stays laced in front. She could be naked in minutes.

He grabbed her wrist. "Ah, ah."

She scowled at him. "What?"

"That's for me to do."

"Then *do* it. You are taking too long."

"I'm going to take my time," he scolded her, smiling a truly dangerous smile she had never seen before. It did not improve her patience. In fact, it made her feel quite wild. "And I'm going to unwrap you like a present."

"You always took an insufferably long time unwrapping presents," she complained.

"And you tore through paper like a badger. I once saw you bite through a ribbon," he said fondly.

"I want to bite *you*." Everywhere. Immediately.

"I have every intention of letting you."

"I'm not convinced," she sniffed, just to needle him into action. Into touching her, kissing her. *Anything.* "In fact, I think you've changed your mind."

"Brat," he said fondly.

She reached for the placket of his breeches. If he wouldn't touch her, the least he could do was let her touch *him*. He closed his fingers around her wrist and clicked his tongue in disapproval.

"*Keir.*"

"You come first, Sybil. Always. If you don't come, I don't come."

And then he kissed her deeply, thoroughly, even as his thumbs grazed her quim, slipping through her wetness, parting her until she was gasping into his mouth. He was still teasing her. A brush of his fingers, pressing just inside, slipping up and over her bud until she squirmed against him.

And then he released her to finish loosening her dress. She was wet and swollen and panting for breath as the dress was pulled off, then her stays. Her chemise was thin, reaching the tops of her thighs. Her nipples strained against the sheer material, puckering at just the brush of his gaze. "Sybil, do you like this chemise very much?"

She swallowed. "No."

"Are you quite sure?"

"Yes."

"Thank God." His big hands fisted into the chemise and he tore it in half. The sound went straight to her head. She gasped. "It was in my way."

"I've decided I hate all chemises."

He ran his palm up her torso, as if mesmerized. "Your breasts are absolutely"—he dipped his head reverently toward them—"perfect," he continued, around her nipple, sucking it slowly, then with more fervor. Heat shot into her quim with every lick and suckle. Her toes were curling into the coverlet by the time he dragged his lips down her stomach. She wanted to touch him, but he was just out of reach, gleaming and golden.

He pushed her back onto the mattress, pinning her there with one big hand.

And only when he was satisfied that she was going to stay still did he use his thumbs to part her slick folds, licking into her, rolling the tip of his tongue over her bud. Back and forth, licking, sucking, drawing her into his mouth until she bucked and writhed against the mattress and he made a sound of approval against her flesh. She was lightheaded and sweaty and quite desperate.

She was coming apart.

There was no warning—one moment she was desperate and then the trembling heat washed over her in cresting waves that stole her breath. It stole every worry, every thought. Everything that was not Keir and his hands and his mouth and the filthy sounds of his enjoyment.

When she finally collapsed back, utterly spent, he looked up at her from between her thighs, green eyes gleaming with satisfaction. "You look very proud of yourself," she murmured.

"Shouldn't I be?"

"Oh, absolutely," she said, desire feeding desire, even when her muscles felt so soft that she was not sure she could stand.

Luckily, what she had in mind did not require standing.

"My turn."

She pulled at him until he prowled onto the mattress, naked and delicious. His erection speared up, hard and flushed with arousal, just from bringing her pleasure. This man.

She closed her lips around his cock and sucked. He cursed, groaning. She liked him like this, at her mercy, without the trappings and pressures of his title. She always had. She swirled her tongue on the underside of his length, over the tip, and then sucked again, and again, harder and harder. His breaths grew harsh and guttural. "Your *mouth*."

He tasted salty and clean, and he was trying so hard not to lose control.

"Sybil?"

"Yes?"

"You are making me feel quite uncivilized."

"About time."

"Wicked, wicked thing. Come here. *Now*," he demanded, pulling her up next to him and then pushing her onto her back when she took too long to comply. He lifted her knee, surging into the space between her thighs, pressing down over her. He blocked out the firelight, the cold draft at the window, everything.

It was overwhelming.

Too much.

Perfect.

She lifted up against him, opening the cradle of her thighs further until he looked quite feral, watching her as though he could eat her up. The tendons of his neck worked and his shoulders tensed as he held himself up over her. He bent his head to kiss her again, deeply, stroking his tongue along hers as he slid inside her. Her intimate muscles clenched around him. She took a deep breath and relaxed around him, and he slid deeper still, making them both moan. He was everywhere. He was everything.

They clung to each other, meeting thrust for thrust. Chasing every sensation.

"Not yet," he muttered when she closed her teeth around the spot where his shoulder met his neck. He cursed. "Vixen. Not yet."

"Now," she argued, sweat gathering in the hollow of her throat.

"Not until you come again."

"I can't," she babbled, lost to the friction and the stretch of her body around him. It felt so good. He kept his pace, brutal and deep and unhurried.

"You can," he promised, gently domineering. Demanding everything from her. Giving everything to her in return. He reached down between their bodies and stroked her nub, slippery and sure. She moaned. It was too much. Just enough. She was past thoughts. She was nothing but her body, nothing but the heat pooling inside and sparking down her limbs.

When she bucked against him, the rhythm of his thrusts changed, stuttered. "Now," she urged him, just as demanding. "Now, Keir."

He groaned, pulled out as though it cost him several years off his life, and spent into the sheets. There was only the sound of their panting, the pop of the fire. She had never experienced such a violent release, and the world remained quiet, a cold winter's night.

Keir got to his feet, pushing his tangled hair off his face.

She waited for him to reach for his clothes, to walk away. She wrestled with the disappointment welling inside of her.

And he did walk away.

But this time he returned. He didn't drag on his breeches, didn't tuck her back into her dress, gentle but swift. This time he returned with the washbasin and a cloth to help her clean up. Part of her teared up, and she refused to give in. Instead, she wrinkled her nose, intending to save them both from the awkwardness of the aftermath. It was uncharted territory for them. "I can do it."

"Sybil," he said, very seriously, "this is my privilege."

She let him tend to her and tried not to lean into the gentleness of the moment, the possibilities it promised. Because reality lingered, unsaid.

So, naturally, Sybil proceeded to say it.

"Keir?"

"Yes, plum?"

"I will not marry you."

She might *want* to marry him. Quite desperately, actually, if she thought about it, which she refused to do because it was not sensible. She might *feel* different, but she wasn't. Not really. Her circumstances certainly had not changed. Although his had, as he was no longer courting Lady Violetta.

"Keir, are you listening to me?"

"Yes. Of course."

"You are going to wake up in the morning full of honorable intentions and untarnished reputations and honor and all that rot you love so much." More than her. She could feel it. After all of those stolen moments in dark rooms, carriages, against the garden wall. This time was different. Something was changing. Had changed.

But not Society.

Never that.

"Rot?" he said, amused. "You reduce hundreds of years of Society to 'rot'?"

"Easily. All of those rules and protocols are not made to help me at all, despite the claims to the contrary. Women are not gentle sparrows who need tending. I'd much rather have access to my own money than a sonnet about my golden hair." She shook her head. "I am getting distracted."

"Excellent."

"I mean it, Keir. I won't marry you."

"Let's see, shall we?"

CHAPTER SEVENTEEN

IT WAS ONE thing to be told he could not marry Sybil when he was younger, to even say it himself, numerous times, for very different reasons.

It was quite another thing to hear Sybil say it. So plainly, so stoutly.

He did not care for it.

That was an understatement. It made him want to bare his teeth at the world. It was his own fault, and his father's. She was only saying the exact words he had said to her by her bedroom fire after Fortingham's. Like an idiot.

Because he thought he must, not because he wanted to.

Because he had been a coward, afraid of a dead man.

But seeing her in danger, twice in one day, was more than he could handle. And exactly enough to crack the rusty armor his father had forced upon him. It was his fault for letting it remain as long as it had. For choosing anything or anyone but Sybil.

There was no doubt that he had kept her safe from his father by pulling away. But that was years ago, when he was too young to know any other ways to fight. Before he was seasoned. What was his excuse now?

He had not stopped hearing his heartbeat in his ears since she had stumbled into his house talking of abduction. It muffled the litany of his father's voice in his head.

But the sound of that rock crashing through glass silenced it. Utterly.

He had battled it for so long, and now it was strangled, choked. Murdered, as it ought to have been so long ago. He had his own cellars to burn. He should have started there.

He couldn't change the past. But he would damn well do everything in his power to change the future.

Sybil sat up, the sheet slipping off her shoulder. She was magnificent, soft and ample, heavy breasts and wide hips and wider grin. He was never going to get his fill of her. He had known that since she first called to him through the crack in the garden wall.

"Why do you look like that?" she demanded. "I just told you I would not marry you. You ought to look relieved. Not stubborn. And pompous," she muttered.

"I do not recall proposing." He would, of course. Would have at that very moment if he thought she would say yes. But first he had to convince her that he could be trusted. That he was strong enough. Truly honorable, not just the pap that they spouted to make themselves feel bigger. Sybil was right about that.

"Oh. Well, that's true. But I know you."

She did know him. And he knew her just as well, no matter the time or distance that had lapsed between them.

How had he survived it?

He knew enough, at least, not to push. She would expect him to put his honor above all else, her reputation. Society.

Hang Society and the honor of his family name.

It felt so good to think it, just once, *finally*, that he nearly laughed.

She stared at his grin, which he knew must make him look cracked. "Keir?"

"And just think of the trouble you could cause as a marchioness. Burn Mayfair to the ground, love. I don't care. I'll carry the matches for you. No?" But he could see that she was tempted. He would take it. "How about an agreement, then?" he asked. "I promise that when I propose to you, it will have nothing to do with reputations and *all that rot.*"

Her eyes were narrowed, suspicious. Beautiful. *"When?* Not *if?"*

"When," he confirmed, very firmly. "Or you can propose to me, if you like. And I'll tell you a secret. I will say yes." Had he ever felt lighter than right now?

"You are vexing."

He was still grinning. "I can see that I am still the romantic one between the two of us."

She snorted.

He fell in love all over again.

He would have said so, plans and strategies be damned, but her stomach growled. She pressed a hand above her belly button. He frowned. "You're hungry."

"A bit."

He was already off the bed, pulling on his breeches. He tossed over her dressing gown, which was draped on a chair. She was appallingly messy. It should have annoyed him to no end. Instead, he found it endearing.

He pulled her to her feet when she was not moving as quickly as he liked.

"Keir, I'm hungry, I'm not in danger of expiring."

"Not while I'm around," he agreed. "Are you getting up or am I carrying you to the kitchens?"

She huffed out a startled laugh. "Don't be ridiculous. I'm hardly a waif to be plucked up off the ground."

"Carried it is."

It was one thing to carry her a few paces outside of a gentlemen's club and another to carry her throughout the house and down two flights of stairs.

"You can't be serious," she said, even though she was thoroughly enjoying it. "Put me down."

"Certainly not."

"You'll hurt yourself."

He only raised his eyebrow in that imperious way of his. She shook her head, before resting it on his sturdy shoulder. His arms flexed around her. She dragged her fingernails through the soft pelt of hair on his bare chest just because she wanted to. Because she could. She nearly purred.

"Keep that up and I'll stop right here and take you in this hall. We'll utterly scandalize that portrait of Joan of Arc."

"Believe me, she's already scandalized." Sybil nuzzled his throat, then bit his earlobe. His breath went harsh. "I dare you."

"You are incorrigible."

"Utterly." And this was the easy part of what lay between them. The attraction, the need. The fire. *That*, she understood.

Keir turned his head and kissed her, hard, quick. Possessive. "But you're still hungry, so you'll be fed first."

He ducked under the doorjamb into the kitchen, as if he did this sort of thing all of the time. Maybe he did. Perhaps he had spent all the years they were not on speaking terms carrying women around his house in his giant arms as though they were goose down.

But she didn't think so.

Something had happened in that complicated brain of his when she told him she would not marry him. Some puzzle had been solved.

Marriage was not the answer, of course. He would realize that in the cold light of the morning. She was still a foundling. A spinster. Still referred to as *That Girl*, with a shake of the head, even though she was not a girl and had not been one for some time. Some of that was the persona of her own making. Some of it was not.

But for now, she was the woman who knew that he growled deep in his chest and shuddered when she took him in her mouth.

Again, it was enough.

She did not know whom she was arguing with, because the insufferable mountain of a man was not discussing any of it. He was clearly on a mission. He set her down on the long table near the grate, where the fire had fallen to coals, and urged them back to flames. She memorized the way he crouched, the play of muscles under his skin. The material of his breeches tight over his thighs. The light gilding his strong jaw. She wanted to live in this perfect, quiet moment.

The kitchen was not fussy or large, but it was clean and comfortable. There was a rocking chair by the grate, shelves of jars containing staples like flour and salt and boxes of spices, jelly molds, butter stamps, and copper pans hanging on the walls. There was a cat, Parsnip, who eyed them disdainfully for interrupting her rest and stalked away down the hall to the housekeeper's private parlor. It was chilly, but not unbearable. It smelled of smoke and sugar.

"There's cake in the blue tin just there," Sybil pointed out, since she had tried to reach it herself but Keir had immediately turned his head to growl at her.

She still hopped down from the table to fetch the wheel of cheese and the last of the previous day's bread, wrapped in a cloth. Mostly because the stern, disapproving look he sent her never failed to make her tingle.

When the water in the kettle boiled, he wrapped the handle and carried it to the teapot, pouring it over the leaves Sybil had already put inside. She brought out the honey and two clay mugs, not at all the fancy bone china the Marquess Blackburn was used to drinking from. "Finally," he approved. "Something I won't be terrified of snapping in two."

"You know, you are frightfully wealthy. You can replace all the cups in your house. Your father had atrocious taste."

"He really did."

"That ornate clock with the gold and the sapphires?" She shuddered.

"He wanted to have it buried with him."

"You should have obliged him." She did not speak false words of sympathy. She was more sorry that Keir had that man as a father than she was that he was gone. "Apples or plums?" she asked instead.

"Plums," he said. The fire outlined him in gold. "Always. They are still my favorite."

"They are?"

"Ever since you gave me that basket of plums."

Sybil tilted her head. "That doesn't sound like the boy who told me I would never truly understand the demands of a title and that you needed to consider your future."

Keir winced. The rough suggestion of a beard shadowed his jaw, his cheeks. He had not been that boy for a very long time. "I've never said how sorry I was."

"You haven't," she agreed, and although she was much more interested in nibbling her way across his chest, she supposed this was more important.

"I am sorry. So very sorry."

She nodded. "I would rather know what happened. I thought it was grief over your mother, but you never came back, not even months later." She had missed him so much that she had scaled the garden wall more than once, only to stare at the candlelight in his bedroom window and then climb back down into her own garden. And after a while there was not even any candlelight to stare at. "Was it just that you were a lad off to Eton and Oxford and never thought of me again?"

When he looked at her, his eyes were tempest green. "I thought of you every single day."

"That doesn't make sense. It never did and it still doesn't. We were... friends, if nothing else."

"My father did not approve."

She sat back. "Oh." That was not a surprise. She had already known that. There were very few people who truly approved of her back then. Or now.

"He threatened you," Keir explained, voice harsh.

She frowned. "He did?"

"I didn't know how else to protect you. So I went away. I pretended I had outgrown our friendship. He was listening that day at the front door." He rubbed his jaw. "I was an idiot. A cowardly idiot."

"You were sixteen years old," Sybil pointed out. Oh, how she wished, for the first time, that his father was still alive that he might know the justice of the Spinster Society. She was angry, a little disappointed. Saddened for the boy she knew. But also relieved. Finally, an explanation. An answer. "Your father was, and I am not at all sorry to speak ill of the dead, a monster." She remembered every bruise that man had put on Keir growing up.

"Still. I should have fought harder."

"Keir, he nearly killed you more than once as it was. Grown men, earls and viscounts among them, were terrified of your father. Never mind a lad thoroughly under his power."

"We could have run away."

"He would have found us," she said. "An heir to a marquessdom does not just get to disappear. Even without that beast for a father."

"I just couldn't let him hurt you," he said quietly. "He said I was getting too attached. He had a footman watch you for a week, just to prove he could."

She shuddered. "The man really was an ass."

Keir choked on a half laugh. "You were always the only one brave enough to say so. I think he knew it, too."

"I wish you had said something. At least later. When you could." She supposed the man had only been dead a few months now. Sophie ought to be in her mourning blacks. It was telling that she was not and that Keir had not pushed the matter.

"My father's reach was long. Too long."

"Did you really eat those plums? I felt a proper idiot for bringing you fruit."

"It was the only food I could stomach for two days. We had to find a wet nurse after my mother died, and my father was not... quick about it. If Sophie had been a son, there would have been one already waiting, just in case." He stared at the flames. "I didn't know the first thing about finding one. Mrs. Hawkins had to intercede. We were afraid Sophie might not make it."

"I didn't know that."

"As soon as she was old enough, I made sure she was sent away to school. No governess, despite the fact that it's the thing. Anything to get her out of that house." When his hand curled into a fist on the table, Sybil rubbed his knuckles. He glanced down as if surprised. "This is not a night for such a conversation."

"I don't mind."

"I'd rather remind you that there are two more hours until dawn and I intend to make use of every single minute."

CHAPTER EIGHTEEN

LEAVING KEIR STRETCHED out half naked in her bed was possibly the most difficult thing Sybil had ever done.

And that was including the time she had climbed out of the icy Serpentine without any help. But he was sleeping so soundly, the tense lines of his jaw relaxed, that she did not want to disturb him. He had slept with his chest pressed to her back the whole night. He was still here. It was unexpected, even after what he had told her about his father. So she did not wake him, even if she wanted to drape herself over him.

Instead, she just stood there and stared at him for a very long time. An embarrassingly long time.

There had been very little sleep to be had. She was tired, a bit sore, famished.

And it was absolutely worth it.

But she was still a Spinster. Breakfast meetings were part of the system that kept things running smoothly. Or as smoothly as they could, considering the things that they got up to.

Not to mention that she required a trough of tea this morning.

The others were already gathered, including Priya and Pierce. Tea was poured before Sybil had even found her seat. "Bless you, Peter. I left the Copperwhite letters in your study," she added to Priya as she scooped blackberry jam onto a slice of cheddar for her bread.

"Yes, I saw that, thank you," Priya said. "Lady Venetia will be much relieved."

"Any progress on the rock through the window?"

"Sadly, no. We can assume Minos, but unfortunately, I am no nearer to finding out who he is. Or they are."

"I'll find this Alfie today," Pierce promised grimly.

The chandelier rattled slightly overhead. Matilda smirked. "Your guest, Sybil?"

Sybil smirked back. Before she could reply, the heavy footsteps paused, started up again. Keir appeared in the doorway. "Good morning, ladies," he said, cheeks ruddy. "Gallagher."

He was as awkward as it was possible for a marquess with seven houses and the ability to brush the chandelier with the top of his head could be. His hair was tousled, as if he had combed it with his fingers, which he no doubt had. His shirt was creased, cravat missing. A marquess seldom showed himself to the world without the aid of his valet. And never at breakfast in a house that belonged to an unmarried lady. Several ladies. "I've... come to take Sybil for a promenade."

"At ten o'clock in the morning?" Peony asked dubiously.

He shifted. "Er... yes?"

Sybil grinned at him over her teacup, thoroughly amused. He did not know the rules for this sort of thing and was no doubt scandalized. It was very endearing.

"That's odd," Peony added, adding salt to her eggs. "As I heard your footsteps coming down the stairs just now."

"I..."

"You are not light of foot, my lord."

"Peony, stop teasing the poor man," Emmeline said. "He's already looking a little peaked."

"Sit down, Lord Blackburn," Priya said, amused. "Break your fast. We do not stand on ceremony here."

"Have some coffee," Emmeline offered. "I made it myself."

Everyone shook their heads in warning. Even the footman

behind her, and it was not discreet.

"Thank you," Keir said, and accepted the cup she poured for him, incapable of being impolite.

They would devour him whole in this house.

Keir took a sip, swallowed without a wince, and then added cream. Sugar. More cream. And took another sip. Emmeline beamed at him proudly.

"It's like watching lions play with an injured gazelle," Pierce muttered.

"I have rarely been compared to a gazelle," Keir remarked drily.

"You have rarely been with the likes of these ladies."

"That is no doubt true." He piled his plate high with ham and eggs and fried potatoes. "You need more footmen, Gallagher."

"Also true."

Priya huffed out an annoyed sigh. "We need actual footmen, at some point. Not just soldiers roaming the halls. Not that you are not most grateful to have you here, Peter," she added.

"Thank you, Lady Langdon."

"I can get you footmen," Keir said. "Proper footmen. But big, at the very least."

"And I can get more soldiers."

"Excellent."

Priya sat back. "And who, exactly, are you two to make such a decision?" she asked evenly. Too evenly.

Pierce and Keir froze.

"Who's the gazelle now?" Sybil snorted.

Matilda popped her chin in her hand to watch the entertainment.

"I have overstepped." Keir nodded. "I apologize."

"I haven't," Pierce muttered. "And I don't."

Peony whistled. "We don't usually have bloodshed before we have even finished our morning tea."

"Yes, Mr. Gallagher," Priya said, steel in her tone. "Let me pour you another cup of tea."

Priya was well known for the herbs she added to the tea of those she was not pleased with. Herbs to cause drowsiness, cramps. Itchy ears. Violent complaints of the stomach.

Pierce winced. "No, thank you."

"*We* will decide if we need more soldiers," she added, dark eyes flashing.

"Be reasonable, Priya."

"Reasonable?"

There were gasps from around the table. Emmeline and Matilda exchanged wagers. Sybil wondered if she should slide Priya's fork out of reach before she used it to stab her Irishman. She decided to leave it.

Pierce scrubbed a hand over his face. "You know what I mean. I'm worried. Things are escalating."

She sniffed, relenting. "As it happens, I agree with you."

"If you would just—You do?"

"Yes, but if either of you make pronouncements at our table like that again, you'll be barred from the house. I can hire soldiers too, Mr. Gallagher. Just see if I don't."

He kissed her knuckles. As she did not use them to bloody his nose, the matter seemed settled.

"If you've copied all the information you need from the betting book," Sybil said, "I wonder if we should return it? I don't think it will be enough to call him off, whoever he is, but it might buy us a little more time to plan."

Priya nodded. "Agreed."

"I can do it," Keir said. "I'm a member of Fortingham's, remember?"

"But I think we should see the other betting books in Town as well," Sybil said. "They might also be marked. Either way, it will tell us something more."

"Marked?" Keir asked. "Marked how?"

Sybil glanced at Priya, then the others. They only looked back at her, waiting for her verdict. She nodded once. Priya nodded back. Whatever else was happening between them, Sybil trusted

Keir. And he was right, they could use his help. Sybil was obviously not allowed inside the club anymore, and Lord Singleton was not a member. Neither was Pierce.

"This is not a finishing school," Sybil admitted.

"You don't say," Keir replied, dry as decade-old tinder. "I am shocked to hear it."

She wrinkled her nose at him. "Do you want to know or not?"

"Go on."

"We protect the women of Mayfair." When he frowned, she pointed at him. "And if you are about to suggest that is the job of a husband or a father, I will let Priya make *you* a cup of tea."

"I wouldn't dare."

"Clever man," Emmeline approved. "Have more coffee."

"There are too many fortune hunters and lecherous lords in London," Sybil continued. "And very little recourse left to the rest of us."

"No argument there. Men like Eastbourne?" His jaw clenched.

"Exactly."

"Is that why you were in his cellar?"

Sybil nodded. She smiled widely at her friends. "Keir burned it down."

Peony looked impressed for the first time that morning. "Well done, you."

"Eastbourne and Portsmouth and Chiswick do as they please, and it is always the women in their lives who pay. *They* never pay."

"Until now," Keir guessed.

"Until now."

"And the abduction, the rock through the window?"

"We are very effective, my lord," Priya said. "If not quite as secret as we once were."

"And they do not appreciate us." Sybil shrugged. "Which is no great surprise." She used leftover jam on her plate to make the symbol of three dots. "Have you seen a mark like this before?"

Keir studied it a moment, then shook his head. "Should I have?"

"Someone marked Eastbourne and Portsmouth and Chiswick and a few others with this symbol in the betting book. None of the men are good *ton*. It is the only thing they really have in common."

"Right bastards," Pierce agreed grimly.

"Have you heard of a secret society calling themselves Minos?" Sybil asked.

"I'm afraid not," Keir said.

"I am not surprised. You are *not* the type they are recruiting."

"I can ask around."

"In the meantime," Sybil said, "Keir will return the betting book and I will make the rounds of the other clubs and see what I can find out."

"*We* will make the rounds," Keir corrected her. He glanced at Sybil, the other ladies. "Please."

"Better," Priya murmured.

"I should be off." Keir placed his napkin to the side. "I have to see to my sister. She has already scared away three chaperones, and it's only been three days. I shudder to think what she has accomplished this morning while I was not there to welcome the newest victim."

Sybil followed him out of the breakfast room and down the hall to the front door, where the footmen had very helpfully made themselves scarce. He appeared pensive but not surprised. She had expected a lecture of some sort, a recitation of the rules of proper Society. Something about danger and reputations. Outrage. Smugness that he was right all those years ago and she was too wild for Polite Society.

He did not oblige.

"You are not shocked at all, are you?" she blurted out.

"Well, I didn't think you were hosting a needlepointing club, Sybil." He leaned down to press his brow to hers. "I was serious before. There's nothing you can do, nothing *anyone* can say or do, that would make me abandon you again. Not unless *you* asked it of me."

"This is not exactly behavior worthy of an earl's daughter." Or a marquess's wife. Surely he could see that. She might understand why he had acted as he had when they were younger, but he was still Keir. Mayfair was still Mayfair. Society was still Society. He had no idea, not really.

"But it *is* behavior perfectly worthy of Miss Sybil Taunton."

"You are taking this far too well." It gave her hope. Too much hope.

"Did you want to me call for smelling salts? I'm not a boy anymore. And my father can't hurt you," he added sharply. "*No one* will. That's all that matters to me. So, you'll wait for me tonight," he ordered, catching her chin firmly to tilt her face up. "You don't go in there without me."

Sybil rolled her eyes.

He kissed her. Thoroughly. Distractingly. Deliciously.

She bit his bottom lip in retaliation. His grip tightened briefly, eyes flaring.

So she did it again. "Hurry."

SOPHIE SHOWED UP at the front door a few hours later with two young ladies in tow. One of the housemaids at Wentworth House had slipped her the address of Spinster House. She had been asked to do so if any ladies showed up unannounced, especially if they looked nervous. Sophie did not look nervous, but she was known to the household. And the blonde girl definitely seemed nervous. She was bright red and looked ready to bolt. Or faint.

"Jane, do stop wringing your hands," Sophie muttered.

"My mother would kill me if she knew I was here."

"Then do not tell her." Sophie rolled her eyes. "Problem solved."

"Ladies." Sybil stepped aside to let them in, casting a quick glance out of the door. She motioned for their coachman to take the carriage down to the mews. The fewer family crests associated with this house, the better. "To what do I owe the pleasure?"

"Sybil, this is Lady Jane Sweeney and Miss Margaret Reed." Sophie tilted her chin up defiantly even though there was nothing yet to defy. "We want you to teach us."

The footmen drifted away when it was evident the young ladies were not being chased by anyone. "Teach you?" Sybil echoed.

"What you told me in the Park," Sophie elaborated. Her eyes shone. "And how to kick a gentleman properly. Mostly that. I have since discovered that Mr. Pelham was courting two *other* girls. Jane was one of them."

Jane winced, but she did look interested in the idea of kicking someone. Margaret grinned, her black hair coiled prettily under her bonnet. "I punched an earl's son last month, but I bruised my hand. It hurt for days."

"Yes," Sybil said, "I imagine so. It's best to use the elbow in most cases, or the heel of the hand. Come along."

They followed her wide-eyed down the hall, ducking under ferns. "Was that Lord Oliver you punched?" Sophie asked.

Margaret nodded. "I ought to have known not to trust him. He kept reciting Byron to me."

"I thought Byron was all the rage?" Sybil asked.

The dry, and deeply disgusted, expression on all three girls' faces when they turned to her at once was identical. Sybil felt like she was back at home staring down her governess. Judged and found ridiculous. She had to grin. "Oh, you'll all do just fine. Here we are, the ballroom."

"We do not wish to learn the quadrille," Sophie said.

"And Jane's mother has us reciting proper ballroom etiquette before we are allowed a single sip of tea," Margaret said. "It takes a very long time, and the tea always goes cold."

"She says a gentleman would not wish to marry a lady who guzzles her tea," Jane added.

"Your mother is awful."

"I know."

Sybil watched them as they stepped inside the ballroom, still chatting. They fell silent when they realized the dance floor was mostly filled with targets. And an obstacle course. A basket of rapiers sat by the door.

"Oh, now *this* is a ballroom," Sophie exclaimed. "Sybil, you never said."

Margaret nodded. "I like the quadrille," she said. "But I shall like this too."

Jane looked unsure. But also curious.

"It's Jane's first Season," Sophie explained. "And as we are not out yet, we shan't be there to protect her." She lowered her voice. "She's very nice."

"And her mother really is a nightmare," Margaret added.

Jane frowned. "*And* I'm right here." She sighed. "But they are quite right on both counts."

Sybil grinned. "Never fear. You can be nice *and* protect yourself."

"Some of us are much subtler than Sybil," Peony said, dropping suddenly from a rope above their heads. Jane squeaked. "Not *me*, mind you." Peony dusted chalk off her hands. "But others."

"Ladies, meet Peony," Sybil said. "You will hate her by the end of the day, but you will thank her later."

Peony preened a little. "I don't need to be loved," she said. "I only need to be effective." She circled them, focused and slightly unnerving. "Pugilism, I think. Every lady needs to know how to plant a proper facer. And we'll have Priya make up some teas for you in the meantime. But first, you'll run the obstacle course so I can assess your skills."

Jane gulped. Even Sophie shifted uncertainly.

"Oh, you will positively despise Peony," Sybil grinned. "Almost as much as you hate the obstacles." Particularly crawling on their bellies under the wooden platform.

"When was the last time *you* went through the course, Sybil?" Peony narrowed her eyes.

"This week! With you!"

"You threw daggers and climbed a rope and sighed over a handful of letters. That hardly signifies."

Sybil groaned. Loudly.

CHAPTER NINETEEN

"I AM NOT going back to school."

Sophie attacked the fish on her plate as if it had offended her.

As if it was her brother's big head, in point of fact.

Something that she pointed out. Loudly.

Keir had returned home just in time to slip into the dining room and take his seat as his sister came down the stairs. He did not want to have to explain his absence. And so he ate a second breakfast of good, proper tea instead of the acid Emmeline had served him, and a sweet bun.

How different this room was from the other. Here the drapes were heavy, embroidered with gold and tied with matching gold tassels. The cups were as delicate and fluted as if they were made of lily petals. His father had preferred everything to be fragile, especially when his son grew bigger and stronger than he was and struggled to feel comfortable. Crystal beads dangled from every chandelier, the candlesticks gleamed, oil paintings of renowned Montgomery ancestors glowered from the picture rail above several footmen standing at attention, should Keir find himself unable to reach for the salt. He would send half of them to Sybil this very day. Those that looked strong enough. Were clever enough. Good enough.

In contrast, Spinster House, as he was told it was called, was filled with plants and books and daggers hidden in the oddest places. The chairs were sturdy. The earthenware mug Sybil had handed him in the kitchen had made him want to propose right then and there.

Of course, he had wanted to propose when she made that little gasp when he sucked her nipple into his mouth. When she had rolled her eyes at him. When she had dragged her nails across his chest. When she paused to watch him, thinking he was asleep. Every time he looked in her direction, really. That had never changed, only now he could indulge the thought.

And now that he had granted himself permission to look at her, to want her and crave her? Now that he knew the taste of her pleasure in his mouth without rush? His need for her would not be satiated. A frozen river in his mind had shattered to pieces with the parlor window, flooding him with images of Sybil waking up in his bed, walking with him through the park, wearing his ring on her finger. Even when she was also wearing that ridiculous getup as Lord Singleton.

"You're not even listening to me," Sophie complained.

"I don't have to," Keir pointed out, pouring himself more tea. He could swear Emmeline's coffee was still burning in his stomach. "You've said the same thing three times now."

"Because you never take me seriously."

"It's hard to take someone seriously when they put porridge in other people's shoes." He wasn't wrong, but he was also aware that he sounded like a prig. Exactly as Sybil accused him. "You have to go to school, Sophie," he added somewhat helplessly.

"I already know my sums. I know French, a little Italian. I can dance a quadrille and curtsy when the queen requires it. I can ride a horse and embroider a pillow. And I read the newspaper every day, even though I was told it would weaken my eyes and that gentlemen do not like a lady who knows more than they do."

He frowned. "Who told you that?"

"Who *hasn't* told me that?"

"I'll find a better finishing school," he promised.

"If you send me away, I shall just make them send me home again."

"It's not sending you away." Didn't she realize he had no idea what he was doing? Why would she want to live in this soulless, joyless mausoleum? She was better off anywhere else.

Well, perhaps not *anywhere*. That headmistress had deserved porridge in her shoes, and any future teachers would know to be very, very careful with his sister. Because her wildness was no excuse for discourtesy, or worse, unkindness to her.

"You don't have to look at me like that," she muttered, misreading his scowl. "This is my home too."

Not if he could help it. She deserved so much better.

"Your new chaperone will arrive any moment," he told her, changing the subject. "Try not to make this one cry."

"I did not make the last one cry."

"On the contrary, she left here in tears."

"Because she was scared of *you*!"

"Because *you* snuck away and she thought you had fallen in the Serpentine and drowned!"

"Because *she* was a ninny," Sophie returned.

She was not wrong. Not that he would admit it. And arguing with her was not making him sound like a sensible man twice her age. He was grateful when Chevril appeared in the doorway. "A Mrs. Gorse for Lady Sophie, my lord."

"Thank you, Chevril. Send her in." Keir glanced at Sophie pointedly. "Be nice."

Mrs. Gorse was a stout woman wearing a very lacy bonnet and a soft, nervous smile. Keir knew at a single glance that she would be no match for his little sister. Especially when Sophie stood and curtsied perfectly with a smile so sweet it rivaled a Gunter's fruit ice. He groaned. "Good luck, Mrs. Gorse."

Mrs. Gorse began to look alarmed. Smart woman.

He paused as something occurred to him. "Wait, Sophie, where *did* you sneak off to?"

"I wasn't sneaking off. I saw a friend flirting with someone unworthy of her."

He frowned. "And how did you know he was unworthy?"

Sophie lifted her chin in that stubborn way of hers that sent a frisson of fear through him. "Mrs. Gorse, shall we start with a promenade?"

"Sophie!"

Returning the betting book to Fortingham's was, frankly, anticlimactic.

Sneaking a look at the books of the other clubs on St. James was *much* more fun.

As Lord Singleton, Sybil had been relegated to gaming hells and once, memorably, a brothel. She did not have access to the gentlemen's cubs.

Until now.

St. James was a riot of sounds and colors, from the passing carriages and snorting horses, to the music and laughter pouring from bay windows lit with hundreds of oil lamps. Sybil loved it.

She loved sabotaging it even more.

They stepped into the first club, and she tilted her head down slightly, making sure the brim of her hat shadowed her face. Keir was dressed in a greatcoat and Hessian boots, the cravat around his throat white as the snow around them. "Lord Blackburn," he said in that marquess's tone of his, so commanding and cold. With every expectation of being obeyed, as always.

But when he turned his head, he winked at her.

And she came very close to melting into a puddle right then and there, damn the man.

This was the Keir she remembered. *Her* Keir.

The one she could not keep, she reminded herself. Despite what he believed.

His eyes narrowed as if he could read her thoughts.

"And a guest, Lord Singleton," he added. The butler bowed and moved aside with the alacrity only reserved for marquesses and dukes. Perhaps she ought to have made Singleton the son of a duke no one had ever heard of. Then she would outrank Keir. The fun she could have with that.

The club was loud and smoky and smelled of several different types of colognes. The linens Sybil had wrapped tightly around her torso to contain her bosom pinched.

She loved every second of it.

"Come on, you absolute madwoman," Keir said as she grinned at him.

They took a turn throughout the rooms so as not to arouse suspicion by heading straight to the betting book. Sybil accepted a small glass of port from a passing footman, plucked an apple from the sideboard. Nodded to several men she did not recognize but who congratulated her on beating Chiswick in the horse race.

"Bad luck for him," someone chuckled. "His bride never showed to the church that day either."

"Can you blame her?"

Several hands of cards were being played, and there were two billiards tables gathering dripping candle wax from above and coins from lost games. In the time it took to cross the ground floor, Sybil saw three family fortunes lost and one duel narrowly avoided. They made it back to the table that displayed the betting book.

It was chained to the table.

A thin chain, but a chain, nonetheless.

"Are you cackling?" Keir asked.

Sybil turned the sound into a cough. A manly cough. "Of course not."

"Mm-hmm."

Sybil skimmed the book, taking care not to look too interested in its contents.

Keir loomed. He was very good at that.

The usual wagers were recorded: bets on the weather, horse races, betrothals.

She flipped back a few pages, angling herself so that she blocked the book as best she could. She checked again. And again.

"Not a single name with the mark," she muttered. "Botheration."

"After you took down Chiswick and Copperwhite? Are you surprised?"

"A little," she replied. She paused. "This page is missing." She ran her fingertip along the edge of the page, cut cleanly from its bindings. "Oh, now I am *really* annoyed."

OUTSIDE, THE SNOW had been cleared from the pavement, making it easier to walk to the next club than to bother with the waiting carriage. The gas lamplights created yellow pools of light in the night. Sybil pulled the folded parchment from her waistcoat, and a pencil from an entirely different pocket, purely because she could, in order to mark down the club and the fact that someone had reached the book before her. She would keep immaculate notes just in case something was useful for Priya.

And the pockets were a nice distraction from the vexation.

"This waistcoat has *pockets*," she said.

"They all do," Keir replied, taking his good fortune entirely for granted.

"You have no idea, do you? Just how lucky you are."

"For a waistcoat with pockets?"

"You try hanging pockets from your stays or sewing them into the lining of your cloak and then use that tone with me."

His smile was brief, amused. "I am sure I quite beg your pardon."

"As you should. Pocket pig."

He laughed and looked as surprised at the occurrence as she did. She had missed the sound of his laugh. She had missed *him*. Even entwined together, there had been such distance between them. But last night had been different. Perfect.

"I am sure I have never been called that before," he said.

"Not to your face."

"Duly noted."

"Admit it," Sybil said. "You are having fun."

"I am trudging through slush with snow falling down the back of my collar."

"Like I said. Fun."

"I would have more fun if you married me."

She stumbled to a stop so quickly that her boots skidded on a patch of icy slush. Keir calmly caught her by the back of her coat and righted her.

"You can't just say things like that!"

"Why not?"

"You know why."

"I do not," he said, firmly. "I understand that I must earn your trust."

"You are a *marquess*."

"So it says on the coat of arms."

"And you are infuriating."

"I'm not sure it says that. Though my Latin is rusty, I admit."

"Keir. You cannot make light of this. You will marry someone… proper."

"You are an earl's daughter."

"An *adopted* daughter," she reminded him. "And far from proper. You know that better than most."

"I don't care," he said stubbornly.

"You used to. And you will again. The *ton* thinks I am too much."

"The *ton* can go hang."

"*You* once told me I was too much," she reminded him archly.

"*I* was an idiot." When he noticed she practically had to skip to keep up with him, he shortened his strides. "The truth was, *I* have not been enough."

That last splinter of ice she had nurtured to protect herself began to melt.

Blast.

Luckily, this was not the time to discuss it.

"You know what I do with the Spinsters now," she could not

help but add. "That wouldn't change."

"I know."

"I've taken down several men, you know. Friends, maybe."

"They were no friends of mine," he said, affronted. He paused. "Although I admit I was polite enough with them in Society, and that… does not sit well."

"You didn't know."

"I knew many of them were not good men. I'll do better, Sybil," he said quietly, seriously, and she believed him. "I can promise you that."

"I DIDN'T KNOW you were a member here," Sybil said moments later, when they stopped in front of a bay window gleaming with candlelight.

"I'm not. I asked for a week-long trial this morning."

"Do they do that?"

He shrugged. "They do now."

"Lord Blackburn," the butler greeted them immediately. Warmth and loud chatter enveloped them. The clubs were all the same. Where was the knife-throwing target? The obstacle course? "Welcome, welcome, your lordship." He snapped his fingers at a nearby footman. "William will take your coat, your hats."

"Just a tour tonight, thank you," Keir said smoothly. If Sybil took off her hat, her pinned hair would be obvious to all. "We'll have a wander. And a brandy, if you please."

The footmen took off as though a race had been declared.

"The card tables are that way, and the billiards, of course," the butler said. "The front room is generally reserved for a quieter guest. The dining room is right through there. Our chef specializes in French delicacies."

"Naturally."

It took some time to shake off the butler, who was very proud of the club, down to the building itself, which had stood since the time of King Henry VII. Sybil learned more about plinths and pediments and porticoes in ten minutes than she had in all her time with several governesses. Finally, he was called away by a member.

The book was like the others, leather binding well worn, spine cracked with use. Ink splatters.

And two more missing pages.

Still so many questions. Too many questions. Very few answers.

It was irksome.

Keir glanced down from where he was surveying the crowd like a captain on the deck of a ship, scouring for danger. He watched her reach for the quill. "What are you going to do?"

"I am merely adding a wager."

Lord Singleton wagers Lord Blackburn that he weds first.

"If I can't cackle, then you can't growl," she muttered at Keir.

"The hell I can't." He scowled. "I'm taking the bloody book."

"You can't."

"I think you'll find I can."

"You'll give us away. This is our only leverage." She tried to nudge him away, and when he would not budge, she kicked his ankle. "I'm tired of waiting."

And then, for good measure, she added three dots next to Lord Singleton's name.

CHAPTER TWENTY

"Y OU SHOULD HAVE marked my name," Keir muttered for the third time. "Not yours."

They were warmly ensconced in the carriage. Sybil was feeling quite pleased with the evening's work. Keir, less so. She snorted. "No one would ever believe that Lord Blackburn, Marquess of Decorum and Dignity, would keep company with such men. But they don't know Lord Singleton well enough to make that judgment."

"I don't like it."

She patted his thigh and tried not to be distracted by the feel of his warm, solid strength. "Cheer up, this might not work at all."

"If only that were true. Your plans always work, in some way or another."

She beamed at him. "I've missed you."

He smiled, though the lines of worry between his brows did not budge. "I've missed you more." He rubbed a hand along his jaw. "I do not like it, but I have to go home tonight for Sophie. I am very sure her newest chaperone did not last the day."

"I did not care much for governesses and chaperones either," Sybil said with some sympathy. "They quit at an alarming rate."

"She will have to get used to it until she is back at school."

"She does not care much for school either," Sybil reminded

him gently.

"She does not. But you cannot always get what you want. Even as a Montgomery."

"Which would be reasonable advice if Sophie wanted a unicorn. All she wants is to be with her brother."

Keir stared at her. "She scoffs at everything I say."

"She is sixteen and scoffs at everyone. Not to mention, you do say a great many things that are scoffable."

"Thank you so much, Lord Singleton."

"You're very welcome, Lord Blackburn." She sighed, shaking her head. "You really don't see it, do you?"

"Are you about to call me a pocket pig again?"

"Sophie gets herself sent down from school so she can be with *you*, you big, rock-headed lummox."

"She does not like me."

"She loves you."

"She cannot possibly live in that dour old house. It's not good for her."

"It's not good for you, either."

He shrugged. "I'm used to it."

"That's the problem," she insisted. "The house is exactly as it was when your father lived there. He haunts it far too comfortably. But it's not his house anymore—it's yours." She meant every word and was a little disgruntled to find they applied to her as well. "I escaped that cellar. And you escaped your father. We need to act like it."

He exhaled slowly. "You are annoyingly wise, Sybil."

She flashed him a grin. "I also find it annoying."

"I don't know the first thing about raising a sixteen-year-old girl."

"You'll learn. She's nearly raised; she just needs her big brother around. The rest will sort itself out."

"You sound very sure."

"I am. And if not, you can send her to Spinster House."

"The soul shudders," he teased.

"Doesn't it? But for God's sake, get someone in there to re-decorate. And get rid of that ugly clock."

"And the petal-thin teacups."

"The crystal swan in the ladies' retiring room."

"There's a crystal swan?"

"It's hideous. And the size of a large dog."

"It's the first thing to go," he assured her.

"Good. It has painted eyeballs. It gave me nightmares."

"When were you up there?"

"When your father had those long, boring suppers and you snuck me in the back door. I might not know the fancy front of the house, but I am well acquainted with the back."

"I'd forgotten about that. We stole the frosted cakes."

"They were delicious." She lowered her voice conspiratorially. "I snuck one under his pillow once."

Keir smiled slowly. "I don't remember that."

"He had just sent you away to school. I was cross."

"He ought to have known not to make you cross."

"One of the maids told my mother's lady's maid that it took weeks to get rid of the ants." She sat back, as proud as she had been at twelve years old. "He was furious."

Keir frowned out of the window as the horses turned toward Mayfair. "I am loath to leave you alone tonight."

"I am hardly alone. Between Pierce's men and the footmen you sent, we are entirely out of room. It's very crowded. Peony is not amused."

"It's not enough."

"It's more than enough. Anyway, Minos does not know that Singleton and Sybil are the same. No reason for the society to come for us tonight."

"Except they came for you last night. And the day before."

She shrugged. She might be concerned for the safety of her friends—and her own—but this Minos Society did not get to win. They did not make the rules. And she would not obey.

She would meddle and meddle and meddle until they fell

apart like moth-eaten lace. Insubstantial. Weak.

"If you came home with me, it would not be an issue," Keir said softly, barely loud enough to be heard over the rattling of the carriage wheels beneath them. His breath misted in the air even with the warmth from the heated and wrapped bricks at their feet.

Sybil shook her head. "Now you are just being absurd."

"I am entirely serious."

"Keir, even a spinster on the shelf, such as I am, cannot swan about flagrantly breaking rules like that. Not without consequences. You of all people know that. Even if I snuck in and out, there are risks."

"Such as a hasty marriage."

"Exactly."

"Sybil, I *want* those consequences. That is a risk I am entirely comfortable with you making. Unlike challenging powerful men who are hunting you."

He was so serious. So handsome. So *Keir*. Her stomach dropped but her pulse picked up. Her body was as confused as her mind.

"Let me convince you," he added. It was tempting to let him try. She had never wanted anything more, in fact.

Instead, she sighed. "Have your coachman take us to Seven Dials. Or as near as he dares."

His eyebrows shot up. "Why?"

"Please, Keir."

"As you wish."

SEVEN DIALS WAS a crowded warren of narrow streets, houses barely holding each other up, the sky crisscrossed with lines of laundry. It teemed with residents who lived too many to a room, sometimes without a window or candle between them. Clean drinking water needed to be fetched from a well that was decidedly not clean. Safer and easier to drink at one of the gin mills or the flash houses that were a combination of pub, brothel, and criminal den. There was theft and violence—but no more than in Mayfair, as Sybil had discovered.

It was crowded, stinking of coal smoke and urine and the Thames and refuse. And it was cold, always in danger of burning down or falling down.

And for years, it had been Sybil's home.

She took Keir to the alley now because she did not know how else to explain it to him.

There were so many versions of her. How to explain it when sometimes she could not explain it to herself? He had seen the truest version of her for so many years, but it had not been enough. And anyway, these other parts were real too. They were important. The spinster, the governess, the ill-treated companion, Lord Singleton. The flighty, messy adopted daughter. The street urchin.

Sometimes, it was a little complicated being Sybil Taunton.

Sybil Smith, as she was before the Tauntons.

It was a crowded business.

And it had started here. In a one-room flat with a window. Then a smaller room without a window. And finally, after her nan died of the same fever that claimed her mother, the alley.

And she was lucky.

Some part of her felt guilty that she had escaped. Had been plucked at random like a flower from the roadside. There was no rhyme or reason to it. She could have ended as a pickpocket, a prostitute. Or died of hunger long before that. It made her head hurt to think about it too long. Her chest ached.

Amandine always said the reason was that Sybil was her daughter, but it had taken her some time to find her, and it was as simple as that.

Sometimes, it was.

And sometimes she woke from hazy dreams of a grandmother she barely remembered, of her gray shawl. The sounds of coughing and dogs barking and the time she had burned her toes against a fire barrel because they were so cold she was afraid they were going to fall off. No one lived in the Dials because it was comfortable. Because it was safe. It was just *there*. And too often, that had to be enough.

Most houses did not have the means for cooking, no grate, no coin for coals. Definitely no ice box. But there were always street carts, selling meat pies, toasted muffins. She found one selling hot baked potatoes and handed him coins and a request to bring a potato to every child in the alley. She made the request several times a week, but he did not recognize Lord Singleton, only Miss Taunton. And he warned her every time that it was not safe for her. "Thank you, Tom."

Keir had not spoken yet. He was too intent on watching her, while keeping an eye on the pickpockets who had spotted two flash culls from Mayfair with more money than sense. Even if one towered over everyone and looked as though he could crush a man's skull with one hand.

"He's no goldfinch to rob. I wouldn't risk it," Sybil warned, street cant returning. He was welcome to her coins, but she needed the list of names and those curious numbers to stay in her pocket. "Tell your Captain Tom." She remembered the gangs of Seven Dials—even the children had their own. They had named themselves the Sixes and Sevens. And their Captain Tom was an older boy of twelve who protected them as best he could. She had tried to find him years later, but with no success.

One of the pickpockets blinked at her use of street cant in surprise, took in the width and breadth of Keir, and melted back into the shadows.

The rookery throbbed with sound at all times of the day and night: songs being sung, fights being fought, babies crying, dogs barking, shouts, threats, laughs. Sybil stopped at the mouth of the alley she knew best. Keir might be the size of a standing stone and she might be quick on her feet, but it wasn't wise to wander the Dials. It wasn't wise to stop too long in one spot, either.

"This is where I come from, Keir. And I'm not ashamed of it. There's no shame in surviving, and that's what everyone in the rookeries is trying to do. But the *ton* think differently. A girl from the gutter does not marry a marquess."

There. It had to be said. Out loud. And right here, where the snow had already turned to muck and puddles gleamed with garbage. Where eyes watched them warily from doorways.

Keir turned slowly to pin her with his gaze.

"Did you think I would see this and be shocked? Disgusted?" he demanded. "Do you think so little of me?" He made a sound of frustration. "Of course you do—why wouldn't you? I was an ass."

"I'm not here to make you feel guilty," she said. "I know who your father was. That's hardly your fault."

"And I know who *you* are."

"Do you?" She had to laugh. "Because sometimes *I* don't even know who I am."

"Then I'll tell you, shall I?" he said, nudging her away and down the street to a safer corner, where the carriage waited. "You are the bravest, kindest woman I know. You are appallingly messy. You steal the covers. You do not share cake. And I love you for it. All of it."

The ice in her chest that had started melting earlier when he told her she was not too much, that he had not been enough, was gone now. She wasn't cold even with the snow crunching under her boots, with her ankle aching.

"You can't just turn your back on Society," she said quietly. "I know you too, Keir."

"Of course I can. Sybil, I followed those rules and became an insufferable prig to protect you. And then you were abducted. That rock through your window could have been a bullet. I'm going to keep protecting you, but I'm going to love you too, damn it. And Society can adapt or they can go hang."

"It's not that simple." She waved her hand, encompassing the alleys teeming with dirt and desperation behind them.

"It's even simpler. I love you. There *is* nothing simpler."

He sounded so sure.

She wanted it to be enough.

"You're scared," he realized. "My little rebel, who never found a rule she did not relish breaking, is scared."

"I'm not scared."

She was terrified.

He smiled briefly. The ass.

"I will have you any way you choose, Sybil. I'm not ashamed of you. I am tired of hiding. I want the world to know you are mine and I am yours. But it's enough that *you* know it." He opened the carriage door. "For now."

CHAPTER TWENTY-ONE

THE NEXT DAY, Lord Singleton received a message.

Sybil had been paying a footman at the Clarendon Hotel for several months now to pretend that Lord Singleton rented rooms there when he was in London. Thus far, it had not proved fruitful.

But as of today, it was worth every shilling spent.

She was in the Fern Parlor battling a plant for a spot in the sunlight, that struggled to pierce the clouds and the coal fog and the thick window glass. Priya muttered over her notebook, a cup of tea spiced with cinnamon and cardamon steaming beside her. Parsnip the kitchen cat was entrenched with her own battle with the ferns.

"Did you know that Chiswick, Abbot, *and* Copperwhite were in debt?" Priya asked.

"Rather common in Mayfair," Sybil replied.

"Yes, but we are talking thousands and thousands of pounds. Enough to make a man desperate."

"And a man both dishonorable and desperate is never a good combination."

"No, indeed."

One of the new footmen stepped inside the parlor and paused. "Miss Taunton? Are you in here?"

"Take a sharp right at the potted lemon tree and then straight on into the ferns."

He popped out between two fronds. "A message for you, miss."

"Thank you. Do you need a map to get out again?"

"I can manage. I believe." He did not sound certain as he turned on his heel and fought his way free of the jungle.

Sybil broke a simple wax seal with no recognizable crest. The paper inside held an even simpler message: *Midnight. Come alone. Minos.* And an address.

"I left Sophie and her friends in the ballroom with the knives," Peony said, marching into the parlor in search of tea. "They are improving apace. But none of them can swim worth a damn." Her hair was damp, wrapped in a turban, barely visible above the bank of plants near the sideboard. "Why is Sybil making that sound?"

"She just received a message," Priya replied. "Everything all right?"

Sybil pushed through the leaves, ignoring the horrified clicking of Priya's tongue. "A message from the Minos Society."

Priya and Peony turned their attention on her at once, sharp and vengeful. "Oh?" Priya said.

"For Lord Singleton."

"Oh!"

"There's another word here, in the corner. Ariadne."

Peony rolled her eyes. "Is that a password?"

"Must be."

"Amateurs."

Pierce poked his head into the room. "We found four chaps named Alfie," he said without preamble. "One is an old man who likes to smash his cane into the culls who prey on the women working in Covent Garden. I gave him a blackthorn cane like they use back home. Does much more damage."

"And the others?" Priya asked.

"The others are exactly the types to be hired in a pub by a man they don't know for nefarious deeds."

"That's... too many."

"Agreed. We have questioned them all, and your Alfie, I believe, is all of seventeen years old and is in way over his head."

"What did he say?" Sybil asked.

"Nothing helpful. He was hired by his friend's uncle. No names. Paid in coin."

"The uncle?"

"Conveniently out of town."

"So they know enough to be scared of this Minos Society," Priya guessed.

"Aye. I've got men at the pub and the flash houses in the area."

"I hate it when secret societies are so... secret," Sybil muttered. She waved the invitation like a banner of war. "You take the flash houses. I've got this apartment at the Albany to visit."

"Well, that does not bode well at all."

"For *them*," Sybil said grimly. "Because tonight I mean to get some answers."

THE ALBANY WAS a private collection of bachelor apartments in Piccadilly, set off the busy road. The main building, a converted townhouse, was dark brick with white-painted windows. The covered Rope Walk lay behind, flanked by additional buildings. Lord Byron had apartments here, as did any number of titled men who did not wish to be at home either with their parents or with their wives. And, apparently, a secret society.

Also, Peony was somewhere up on one of the rooftops.

Women were not allowed.

Lord Singleton, however, *was* allowed.

Apprehension and a deep desire for vindication and, let us be honest, violence, thrummed in Sybil's blood. She was not sure what to expect, but these were the men who had tried to abduct her. Who had tried to bring real harm to her friends. Who were responsible for the ill treatment of any number of women besides.

It was not very surprising that it should all be headquartered at one of the most fashionable addresses in London.

Sybil crossed the courtyard and followed the Rope Walk to one of the new sets on the ground floor, near the end. The sound of carriage wheels and late-night carousers drifted from the next street over, but otherwise it was quiet.

Not a good sign.

For one thing, she was not particularly fond of quiet.

For another, Pierce was meant to be here with several of his men. Peony was in place, but where were the others? She would glean as much information as she could, but she did not know how many members waited inside. She could hardly take them all on, even as Singleton. But when else would they get a chance to get the members gathered in one place?

She could not afford to wait any longer.

"Psst," Peony hissed. "Where is everyone?"

"I don't know," Sybil admitted without turning to look at her friend, lest it give them away.

"I don't like it."

"Me neither."

"I did see Keir," Peony said. "He went around back."

Sybil nodded. "I guess this is it."

"Don't die."

"Likewise."

When Sybil finally knocked on the door, a large man holding a cudgel answered. He wore a rough coat, a rougher expression.

"I have an invitation," she said.

"Password," he barked at her.

Passwords. She was embarrassed for them. Secret societies should be more creative by now. She stifled a peevish sigh and lowered her voice. "Ariadne."

Honestly.

"Go on in."

That was when she realized she recognized his voice. He was one of the men who had grabbed her off the street.

The urge to drive her elbow into his nose was strong. *Very* strong.

"Here's your mask. Put it on," he added.

She was already wearing a disguise, and his name was Lord Singleton. But she took the half mask and tied it under the brim of her beaver-crowned hat.

The door opened into darkness, and she forced herself through it, reminding herself that she had three daggers on her person, and Peony. She knew her friend was at her back—or, more accurately, somewhere up high, her rifle trained on the men below. Sybil did not look up.

And Keir.

A single candle burned to show her the way to the main room. It smelled of roasted lamb and incense. The fashion for all things Classical had been indulged, which she supposed she ought not be surprised at, considering they had named themselves for an ancient Cretan myth. The white columns at the front of the Albany were echoed here, holding up the ceiling like a Grecian temple. There was a low table in the center with an oil lamp illuminating bowls of fruit and wine and baskets of bread with hard cheeses.

Around the table were guests wearing the usual fashion of a man-about-town, along with masks and cloaks, but they clearly knew each other. She could spot the other two new recruits from the way they sat quietly, eyes wide behind their masks, without a cloak as she was.

It was like any other gentlemen's club, if not for the undercurrents, the venue. The things they did.

The man who stepped out of the shadows was also wearing a mask. There was nothing about him to recognize—his coat was like any other, his cravat white, his boots polished. His cloak thick and black. He wore no rings, had no scars.

The others came to attention, although coming to attention in such a group mostly consisted of affected expressions of ennui, leaning against the wall, setting down a terracotta amphora painted with a depiction of the labyrinth and King Minos. It was filled with red wine. It was also well over two thousand years old. Sybil had an antiquarian friend who would have wept at the desecration of such an ancient artifact. Not wept. Raged.

Sybil stood very still, waiting.

The man met her eyes. As he did not immediately shout at her to be removed, she could assume her disguise stood. Two more men joined him, unmasked, massive, armed. Protection. And bullies at a glance.

"Do sit down." The man half bowed. "I am Minos. We are all Minos. That is how we protect each other."

That was how they got away with every crime and wrongdoing. Lord Portsmouth had a long list of people from Parliament to the courts to the ballroom whom he blackmailed to cover his tracks. It was how he had gotten away with murdering his wives when they did not produce an heir.

Until the Spinsters.

Kitty, to be exact.

"Three of you have been invited to join us because you know someone like us or you show promise to be someone like us. An asset."

And yet something nagged at her all the same.

Sybil's palms started to sweat. It had felt like playacting before, with passwords and bored aristocrats, but a shiver went down her spine. She knew better than to underestimate a bored aristocrat. It only felt like playacting because they could afford for it to feel like playacting. There were already too many women in their lives who knew this was not a game.

"We have been keeping an eye on you."

The marks in the betting books.

"We know what you've done, what you want to do. And that is why we can help each other. Especially now."

"Why now?" someone asked.

"Because we are plagued by the Spinster Society."

Someone else barked a laugh.

Sybil did not much feel like laughing.

"Ape leaders? Who cares about them? They are hardly a match for us." This from a man Sybil was positive she could best in a bout of fisticuffs. Better yet, a duel.

"They are interfering," Minos said tightly. "We can already no longer use the betting books to send messages. It is too convenient that Chiswick and Abbot and Copperwhite were found out just this month alone."

Was he someone they had personally foiled? Sybil would have to go over Priya's lists again.

"And I want them stopped."

"So stop them," Sybil called out even as her heart raced. "If this society is so powerful as to be worth our time, prove it."

"It's for *you* to prove yourself," he snapped. "They have thinned our numbers, I'm not too proud to admit it. But it stops now. The Season is about to start, and we cannot have them in the way."

"Stop them?" an older man echoed. "I'm not keen on murdering some wallflower."

"Why not? You were perfectly keen on murdering that housemaid."

A hush, a few mutters.

"That was an accident!" he insisted.

"Of course it was," Minos said.

"We have warned them, but they are unreasonable. They are meddling. Put a stop to it."

"How?" Sybil asked, mouth dry.

"I do not care. Do what you must. You help us, we help you."

Bloody hell. He was all but putting bounties on their heads.

"Did you hear that? Sounded like growling."

"Stray dog. Don't be so feeble."

"How are *you* going to help us?" One of the other new recruits asked. It was not a challenge. He was eager to know.

"Money. Witnesses, protection. Doctors who don't ask questions. Suffice it to say that we are putting things back to rights."

Like hell they were. Sybil clenched her fists.

"How much money are we talking about?"

"As much as you need."

The man beside the recruit laughed. "He needs a lot. He's the worst card player I've ever seen."

"You all have titles and will inherit superior ones in due time. Minos can make you even greater. Prove your loyalty. Bring us your sacrifices, as Athens brought Minos their people for the Minotaur."

Rage shivered through Sybil.

They were not sacrifices.

They would never be sacrifices.

"But we need funds to be effective, personally and for the society. The Season will be ripe with debutantes and heiresses. Find one. Admission to this Society is steep."

"I'm not getting *married*. Tied to one chit?" Sybil recognized that voice as well. Lord Coxwell? Lord Campbell? Some name that started with a C.

"Don't be so banal. Don't make us doubt your commitment. Marry and you are free to do as you like without the eyes of the dowagers on you. Marry *well* and you can do *anything* at all. Eastbourne and Portsmouth had the run of Britain until those damned Spinsters."

"This is absurd. I was told there would be women and wine," Lord C argued. "Not this claptrap." He pushed his hood back. "I don't need *your* help. And when my father hears—"

Only he did need someone's help.

As evidenced by the dagger currently sticking out of his back. He gurgled in shock, then pain, before crumpling. No one moved to catch him. A few of them, like Sybil, were frozen. Too many were smiling. Arrogant. Unmoved by the blood and the choking gasps of a dying man.

Sybil finally took a step toward him, but it was too late.

"Anyone else?" Minos asked.

The silence was palpable. Edged with excitement, fear. Potential.

"This is a secret society, and we take our oaths seriously. We won't be undone by weaklings or spinsters."

Sybil's breath was loud in her ears. No one spoke. Blood pooled on the rug, creeping closer and closer to her boot. It smelled coppery, like wet, rusty coins. She fought back a gag.

"We've made a list of suitable quarry. Memorize it. There are fortunes to be had, gentlemen. Don't disappoint us." Minos smiled. "And one more thing."

Well, that was never a good sign. What came after the show, after the flash and pomp, was usually the most important part.

And if the show was outright murder? Not encouraging.

"Get the Spinsters under control. Marry them or murder them, I don't much care. As she helped take down Eastbourne, you can start with Sybil Taun—"

Sybil barely had time to react. And he did not have time to elaborate.

At the sound of her name, a gunshot cracked the air.

A bullet tore through the room, leaving behind a shattered window and hitting Minos in the foot. He screamed, blood spattering. He toppled to the side, caught by one of his men while the others froze in panic. Not so smugly arrogant now. Not so thrilled by the violence when it was not their doing.

Only one of the members stayed calm. He stood slowly, easing out of the pathway of the window in case another bullet followed the first. It didn't. He waited. Watched.

Sybil watched him in return.

As best she could. As Minos was carried out, some of the members threw themselves to the ground, covering their heads. Wine spilled from the amphora, dripping onto the carpet with the blood. There was a great deal of shouting and panic.

But they kept their masks on.

Sybil snatched the list of suitable heiresses and darted toward the window.

Hands gripped her and hauled her out into the cold.

CHAPTER TWENTY-TWO

W HEN KEIR TUCKED Sybil against his chest, she punched him so hard in the ear that it rang painfully, and then hissed at him when she finally recognized him. "You will blow my cover." She blinked at the hunting rifle tucked under his arm. "That was *you?*" She shook her head and smacked his chest. "Put me down before someone sees."

He hadn't even realized he had hauled her clear off the ground. He only wanted her safe. He set her down. Reluctantly. Every instinct insisted he toss her over his shoulder and run for safety.

They had spoken her name inside that room. Unacceptable. While she had been inside not three feet away, a dead man at her feet.

He began to sweat despite the frigid bite of the wind.

He would have shot into the room earlier, but there was no clear vantage point, no way to know for sure that he would not accidentally hit Sybil in the uncertainty after the man had choked on his own blood. These men were clearly unpredictable.

"Keir?"

"Can we get away from the apartments full of men who want to hurt you? I might start sweating blood soon."

"I'd forgotten how dramatic you are." She said it lightly, but her teeth were chattering.

"Sybil."

"I don't know a Sybil. I am Lord Algernon Singleton."

"Algernon," he echoed, fighting a smile. She could always do this to him, tie him up in tangles and still make him want to smile. Particularly as he knew it would help her more than the kind of raging he desperately wanted to give in to. "That's a terrible name."

"My mother gave it to me!" She exclaimed with false offense.

"I've met your mother. She has much better taste than that."

Sybil muttered something under her breath, but at least she was moving *away* from the dangerous apartment. He would shoot them all if he had to, but it seemed a bit messy. And Sybil might object. But only because she might want to do the shooting herself.

"Can you walk faster?" he asked.

"Not without drawing attention to myself."

He swore. "I have a carriage at the end of the walk." Luckily, it was not far at all.

And yet still too far.

Of course.

Because nothing was simple with Sybil.

And he loved that about her. He was going to have to learn several more forms of combat just to keep up.

He was almost cheerful about it until there was the sound of a footstep. Just a scuff.

He shoved Sybil toward the carriage, using his wide back to block anyone who might have her in their sights. He had no idea if those men suspected her or if they were all running blind after the shot he fired.

He just knew he had not fired the second shot. The one that clipped the walkway behind them in a spray of cobbles and ice.

"Time to go," he said, and all but tossed Sybil into the carriage. He swung the rifle back up.

"Don't shoot Peony!" Sybil hung out of the doorway. "She's on the rooftop to your left."

He glanced up to see the other woman running along the roofline, slipping once, regaining her footing, and sliding down a drainpipe. She landed like an acrobat from Astley's Amphitheatre.

These women really were terrifying.

"Get in," he ordered Peony, all but tossing her inside as well. She yelped, landing on Sybil. He shut the door and banged the roof. His coachman, Arthur, having already experienced the chaos that was Sybil, pulled into traffic as quickly as he could.

Keir sat back and tried to convince his heart that it no longer needed to be lodged inside his throat. Sybil was safe. Peony, bless her soul, was also safe, pistol in hand. "Someone was following you," she said. "I think."

"You think?"

"I felt it was prudent to shoot at him just in case."

Keir wondered if she would get the wrong idea if he bought her flowers. Many of them.

"Is that a warming brick?" she asked Sybil. "Share it, you ingrate—I'm more than half frozen from lying on the roof."

Sybil moved over. "Why were you on the roof? I thought you had set up in the apartment across the walk?"

"I did, but the occupant came home early. With two women. And another gentleman. It was a bit crowded."

"They were probably too busy to notice you."

"I decided not to take that chance. There are some things I cannot unsee."

They sounded unbothered by the evening's event, although Keir knew that to be untrue. Sybil's fingers were tangled together, knuckles white. He himself was so on edge that it was a wonder his back teeth had not cracked from the clenching of his jaw.

Sybil pulled off her mask and lifted her eyebrows at him. How did she manage to make an ordinary hat and frock coat look so dashing? "You shot him."

"I did not like the sound of your name in his mouth." His jaw clenched again.

"So you shot him in the foot?"

"I would have shot him in the chest, but I did not have the right angle."

"I didn't have any angle at all," Peony grumbled.

"Well, you shot that bloke who was following me, so thank you both."

Peony just shrugged, more interested in the rifle leaning against Keir's knee. "Is that a Baker's Pattern rifle?"

"Yes, it is."

"With the rifling grooves?"

"Yes."

She pointed to her double-barrel flintlock. "I can shoot twice with this without reloading, but it does not quite have the same accuracy. I've read Baker's alteration means that the rifle can shoot farther than any other gun!"

"Oh, here we go." Sybil grinned. "Now you've done it."

Peony turned to her. "Thomas Plunkett shot a French general at six hundred paces during the war, I'll have you know."

"Who?"

"He was a rifleman, Sybil. Honestly."

Keir was not sure how they had gone from secret societies, murder, and shooting people, at one of London's most fashionable addresses, to this. He handed Peony the rifle. "Take it. It's yours."

Her eyes shone. She grabbed it. "Really?" She clearly had no intention of giving it back.

"Really."

"Thank you." She clutched it to her chest, running her fingers along the proof mark shaped like a crown on the barrel. "She's beautiful."

"She's poking me."

"Then move. Did you get anything useful from that lot in there?"

"They stabbed a man right in front of me," Sybil said. "They are worse than we thought. But they all wore masks and cloaks. They were only familiar in the way anyone of the *ton* is familiar.

But I did get this!" She waved a piece of paper. "A list of their next victims, which I intend to—"

Sybil went silent.

Keir frowned at her, then followed her frozen, horrified gaze.

Fire reached into the sky outside the window as the carriage rolled to a halt, painting it red and orange. They now knew exactly why Pierce and the others had not shown.

Spinster House was burning.

CHAPTER TWENTY-THREE

I T TOOK TOO long for Sybil to understand what she was seeing.

The darkness pulsated with red shadows, glowing menacingly. Tongues of flame licked out of a broken window of the upstairs parlor. Smoke billowed, burning the air and acrid in every breath.

Fear pulsed through her. Fire could eat the house in moments, moving to Priya's house next door and to the other neighbor, and so on and so on.

She scrambled from the carriage, and when Keir reached for her hand she had the fleeting worry that he would try to stop her. Instead, he squeezed her fingers once and then unwound her cravat, rubbed it with snow to dampen it, and wrapped it around the lower half of her face. "Against the smoke," he said gruffly, untying his own cravat and doing the same with it for Peony, who had left her new and precious rifle in the safety of the carriage.

Pierce was running from the main parlor, ashes in his hair, when they burst inside. "Everyone's out," he said. "Two fires upstairs, two down here. Fire brigade will take too long to get to us. I hope you didn't go into that apartment without us."

"Of course I did. Where's Priya?" Sybil asked, coughing. The sound of the fire racing up the curtains, snapping and crackling, made her heart race.

"Finding more buckets. We're using water from the swimming chamber."

Peony pivoted toward the swimming chamber without another word. Footmen stampeded after her holding buckets, flower pots, a carafe emptied of whisky. The servants had formed a line, passing the water hand to hand. There were enough footmen to deal with the upstairs fires, fewer left for the parlor and the ballroom. By the time Sybil joined them, Keir was outside, shoveling snow into the flames as fast as he could.

She did not know how much time passed, only that it was filled with shouting and fire hissing and muscles cramping and cold wind sneaking in to menace them as they worked. Priya returned with a wheelbarrow of plant pots for water from the greenhouse. The domestic fire engine was filled again and again, the leather hose filling with water. More buckets. More filling of the engine. The flames were rapacious.

A single fire was bad enough, but several started at once was brutal in its efficiency.

And could not be accidental.

The Minos Society had already murdered one of their own tonight. Burning down Spinster House with the hope that they were trapped inside was not below them.

But finally, finally, there was only smoke clogging the halls and the charred remains of curtains and furniture in heaps on the wet floor, and the panting and gasping of everyone trying to catch their breath.

"I think that's done it," Pierce said, wiping his face with a damp cloth.

Keir strode in from the back of the house. His shirt was streaked with soot and torn in one sleeve, angry, burned flesh showing. "Nothing left out back. Not even a spark." His eyes roamed over Sybil as he spoke, making sure she was unharmed. She lowered the cravat around her face and smiled wearily at him, already hoping the medicine baskets scattered all around had not been destroyed.

There were several burns to minister to and rough, hacking coughs to soothe with tea and honey, which the cook sent up from the kitchen. But there were no broken limbs, no loss of life. The house had suffered considerable damage, but it could have been so much worse.

In the heart of a fashionable Mayfair apartment, a dead man was still lying in his own blood.

"This was a coordinated attack," Pierce said darkly. "If we had any fewer footmen or guards about the place, we might not have gotten off so well."

"How did they get in?" Sybil asked.

"They didn't. They threw a flaming bottle filled with lamp oil," he said. "The right bastards."

Peter came down the stairs, hair wet and clumped with ashes. "Servants' quarters are untouched."

"That's something," Priya said. "Thank you, Peter."

"The other bedrooms suffered damage. Yours most of all, Miss Taunton, I'm afraid."

Sybil sighed. She would be upset about her room later. Right now, she was so raw that she nearly felt numb with it. Keir poured brandy into her teacup.

"The Minos Society has truly declared war, then," Priya said quietly. "No more warnings."

"You have no idea," Sybil said. "But you'll be happy to know that Keir shot one of them in the foot." Just for speaking her name. Had that really only been a few hours ago?

Priya smiled grimly through her exhaustion. "I knew I liked you, Blackburn. And a lord with a bullet in his foot will be easy to find."

"I'll go now," Pierce said.

Sybil told them what she had seen and heard at the meeting, which was, unfortunately, not enough. But she had a list of names. Of women who could be warned.

"Those men did have one thing in common that I could tell," she added.

"Their days are numbered?" Keir put in darkly.

"There was much talk of debt. And heiresses and dowries. They want us out of the way by the time the Season starts so we do not interfere." She waved the list.

Keir frowned. "Where are you going with this?"

"I have an idea."

He stilled. "No."

"I haven't told you what it is yet," she protested.

"And yet every hair on the back of my neck still lifted in alarm."

"What do you have in mind?" Priya asked.

"They want us all so badly? Let us bait a trap."

"And you're the bait?"

"Yes."

"And what exactly does that mean?" Keir asked. He was beginning to look a little wild around the eyes.

When she told him, he went pale. Pale enough that she wondered if they had smelling salts in one of the baskets with the knives. Assuming those baskets had not burned, of course. "No," he said, the calm of his voice at odds with the tension across those massive shoulders, the clenching of his jaw. "It's not safe."

Sybil met his gaze.

She didn't need her house burning down around her to know that *he* would always be *home* for her.

"If you're that concerned for the safety of my plan, I suppose you ought to marry me," she said.

He turned slowly, his green eyes glittering, pinning her. "Everyone else heard that, right?"

The others, exhausted, covered in scratches and soot and bruises, grinned.

Keir gripped Sybil's hand and pulled her abruptly to her feet. "Let's go."

CHAPTER TWENTY-FOUR

ONLY SYBIL'S MOTHER could have planned such an elaborate masquerade ball in less than two days.

And only her mother could be assured that the guestlist would respond immediately, canceling all other engagements. It did not hurt that word was out that Sybil was now in possession of a dowry. One of the largest in recent years.

If she wasn't enough to draw the Minos Society out of hiding, her dowry most certainly would be. Not to mention, the event was being held at Priya's house. None of her ledgers and notebooks of secrets were on the property because she was not a fool, but it would be temptation enough.

And if the Minos Society feared exposure, as evidenced by their masks and cloaks, then the Spinsters would unmask them for all to see. In the heart of Mayfair, their preferred hunting ground. Tonight, if all went well.

It had not taken long for Pierce to discover that a certain earl's son, Lord Grant, had been shot in the foot and called for a doctor in the middle of the night. Unfortunately, he had also fled London before dawn on a ship bound for France.

"Are you sure about this, *ma puce*?" Amandine asked. "I have outdone myself, of course, and I am happy to do it, but your father and I know perfectly well that you are up to something."

Sybil hugged her mother, who wore a stunning green gown

and a mask of peacock feathers glued to a handle dripping with crystal beads.

For once, Sybil did not have a mask. It was uncomfortable.

"I'll tell you as soon as I am able," she promised. It was the best she could do. It was already difficult enough to keep Keir calm. He lurked in the shadows of the balcony as guests began to arrive.

"Is he growling?" Amandine asked.

"He does that sometimes."

Amandine twinkled at him over her shoulder. "I like it." She turned back to Sybil. "And you'll let me make the announcement? I want to see Lady Cartwright's face when I release the swans in the garden. Luckily, the weather has learned to behave. Oh, and the white butterflies for your announcement!" She kissed her cheek. "I am miffed this could not be done in my own house, but I must say Lady Langdon has outdone herself with the flowers." Her smile broadened. "So much lilac. Did you know it makes Lady Cartwright sneeze?"

Sybil grinned back. "She sneezes like a poodle."

"She does indeed."

"And you look stunning."

"Yes, I do. Ah, here's your father. Isn't he handsome? I do love a masquerade."

"I feel like a fool," Sybil's father grumbled, crossing the landing to join them. He held up his lion mask, which sparkled with amber spangles and had a mane of matching yarn and fleece that reached nearly to his knees.

"*Tres debonair*," Amandine beamed. "Very elegant."

"I have to be in order to keep up with you," he replied. "You look like a queen, my darling. And Sybil, you are a princess."

"Thank you, Papa." Sybil wore a sapphire-blue gown embroidered with so much silver thread that she gleamed and glittered under the light of the chandelier. Diamonds and pearls dripped from her ears and encircled her throat. It was ostentatious, obvious. White spangled silk feathers had been sewn to the back of her gown, like swan feathers. There were birdcages everywhere. Her mother did like a theme. Particularly one that insulted anyone who looked askance at her daughter.

"You were never an ugly duckling, Sybil, but I hope you make them choke on the swan you've become. Now don't dawdle," Amandine scolded. "It's important to make an entrance, but if you wait too long, no one will notice."

"Impossible," Charles said. "My ladies cannot be ignored. Don't know what you're up to, my girl, but give them holy hell."

"I always do, Papa."

Sybil watched her parents descend the staircase, the banister wrapped with ivy. Garlands of spring flowers draped over portraits, hung by ribbons from the chandeliers. Lilies of the valley, delicate bluebells, perfumed lilac branches in silver urns.

And Keir, waiting behind her. She felt him there, solid and powerful.

The others were in position.

It was time.

SYBIL HAD NOT realized how surprisingly difficult it would be to be the only one without a mask.

All of the other guests hid behind spangles and paint and feathers, turning to watch her descend the stairs. Conversations swelled and softened. The rumor of her dowry preceded her, as planned. If nothing else, her mother's party would be remembered. Lilac sweetened the air, purple and white blossoms already scattered on the floor like stars. There were swans carved from ice, sculpted out of butter on the sideboard. Made of flowers. Dangling from the ceiling so they looked to be floating.

Her mother was not subtle.

The master of ceremonies raised his voice, as though he were announcing someone important. "Miss Sybil Taunton, daughter of Lord and Lady Wentworth." He added the last in case anyone had forgotten. Sybil knew that he had been ordered to do so by her parents. A reminder that they would not tolerate any disrespect.

Sybil lifted her chin and entered the fray, trying not to feel like a minnow in the ocean, watching for sharks. The men of the Minos Society, as well as the other garden-variety fortune hunters, were on the move. She might not be able to see them, but she fancied she could feel the ripples, like water betraying what lurked beneath.

But she was a Spinster.

Not a minnow, not a sacrifice.

Tonight, a swan.

Always a Spinster.

And she had an army at her back, hidden throughout the hastily decorated ballroom. Peony stood behind a cluster of potted trees. Emmeline and Matilda circled the room, alert. Priya glowed in pale yellow, every glance a reminder that she probably knew more about you than you did. The footmen were all armed. Not as armed as the Spinsters, but still armed.

And Keir was with her.

She did not turn to look for him. He would be in the shadows, or pretending to speak to other gentlemen, pretending, pretending. He was tall enough to scan the crowd as it pressed closer.

She might be on display, bait dangling and flashing over the river during salmon running—but she had never been so well protected.

Or so eager to deliver a comeuppance.

Sybil greeted guests, acting shocked and humbled by her dowry. She accepted several offers to dance, two glasses of champagne, which she did not drink. And received an offer to be compromised in the cloakroom and do away with all of this courting nonsense.

The viscount in question, who assured her he had a country house and seven hunting hounds, paused. "Do you hear growling?"

Sybil bit back a smile.

The orchestra, hidden in a jungle of ferns, began to play.

Violins, a cello, a harp. Three flutes. Masked dancers paired together. The group of ladies who approached her were also masked, but she had no trouble recognizing them. She knew their voices, their comments, their sharp little smiles.

"Miss Taunton, felicitations, dear," Lady Shrewsbury said. She was not yet twenty and already a duchess. It lent her a certain social power she did not yet know how to wield kindly. "You must be so relieved."

"I can't think why your parents waited so long," Lady Joan added.

"Yes, poor thing, but finally a dowry to offset your... Well, you know."

"My childhood in an alley?" Sybil asked bluntly, mostly because she perversely enjoyed the way it made them squirm. This was not the way the social game was played. You did not say what you actually meant. You did not engage in a frontal attack. It was all feints and parries, sugar-sweet poison unless you could be sure of privacy. "That I was an orphan? The fact that I stole potatoes so I would not starve?"

The ladies blinked. Fans were fanned with more vigor. Between the blinking and the fanning, they might yet create a wind current. One of the swans floating above them began to circle more quickly.

Sybil continued to stare at them, refusing to drop her smile or smooth over the awkward silence. There were white rose petals under her shoes. "Was there something else you wished to say, ladies?"

A sniff. "We meant no harm, I am sure."

"Don't let a dowry go to your head, Miss Taunton. As you say, you are still a—"

"Miss Taunton," Keir interrupted sharply. "I believe you have promised the waltz to me."

Sybil bobbed a curtsy. "Of course, Lord Blackburn." His legendary icy stoicism seemed to be slipping. His eyes burned, green as will-o'-the-wisps.

"Lord Blackburn, you are too kind to our Sybil," one of the ladies cooed. "Such condescension from a marquess to a… woman."

Keir offered his arm and led Sybil to the dance floor, his jaw ticking. "Since when do they talk to you like that?" he demanded.

Sybil shrugged one shoulder. "Since forever. It's not the first time and it won't be the last time."

"Oh, it's definitely the last time," He said it with quiet menace.

"How formidable," she teased, because kissing him under a spray of lilac and white roses was becoming more and more likely. She could not be distracted. Neither of them could be.

He raised his left eyebrow in that way she loved. "It ruins the effect when you comment on it."

"Does it? Duly noted. *My lord.*"

"Scoundrel."

She felt better now, she realized. Ready.

"It's time," she murmured as the music ended.

Keir's expression went inscrutable. She knew now that it only meant he was feeling too many things at once. He nodded once and brought their waltz to an end at the edge of the dance floor. The chalk to keep dancing slippers from sliding was already smudged. Sybil curtsied. His eyes narrowed. She almost stuck out her tongue, would have were this not such serious business.

Instead, Sybil walked away fanning herself, telling a dowager who tried to stop her that she merely needed a bit of air and a moment to rest.

"Of course, all the excitement!"

That dowager had no idea.

SYBIL FELT BETTER the moment she stepped into the hall. The stifling heat, the masked faces all tracking her, made the back of her neck ache. She would rather jump into the icy Serpentine again. Or attend to Mrs. Farraway. Fight an actual swan.

She nodded to one of her mother's friends, then passed the

ladies' retiring room—which was naturally plastered with Spinster Society flyers.

But the ladies' retiring room was not her destination.

She paused by the door to the side garden, near the stairs down to the kitchen, and felt like an idiot. But she had to be seen, here more than anywhere. She poked her head outside. "Come on," she muttered. "Think of my dowry. Take the bait."

Someone grabbed her from behind.

Success.

"No hard feelings," a man's voice said in her ear. He smelled like wine and snuff. "But I need your dowry, Miss Taunton. We're going to Gretna Green."

He slapped his hand over her mouth without realizing that she was not fighting back and had not attempted to scream.

He was yanked off her within seconds.

Keir tossed him down the stairs, where Pierce waited. "One down."

SYBIL DANCED AGAIN, wandered toward the back gardens, danced some more, stepped outside for another breath of air.

One Minos Society member, two.

And three.

They had taken the bait, and now the Spinsters had quite a collection, all trussed up and gagged in the storage room off the kitchen. Keir had broken a few fingers. Sybil had dislocated a kneecap. Peony tripped three earls just because she did not like them.

Sybil's mother had invited three magistrates to the ball, and Priya had invited three Bow Street Runners. They did not yet know what awaited them.

And if anyone noticed that Keir kept tossing men down the stairs, they did not mention it.

When Sybil returned to the ballroom once more, she was glad to be approached by Lord Bailey. Victor was an uncomplicated friend. "Will you dance?" he asked, grinning up at her from his overly elaborate bow.

"Of course, Lord Bailey."

"Lord Bailey?" He made a face. "Never say you've gone and changed on me? Just because of a dowry?"

She softened her polite expression. "Of course not." They always danced together, had done so for over a year now. Only she hoped he did not think there was a chance between them now. She did not wish to hurt his feelings.

But the dance was pleasant and he did not press or make advances, only jolly comments about the other guests. Keir stood against the wall, arms crossed, scowl scowling. He was not very good at this subterfuge business. Threat and menace boiled from him, so unlike his usual calm that more than one glance flickered in his direction. Appreciatively, it had to be said. He *was* rather delicious when he scowled.

She sent him a bright, cheerful smile. He only shook his head, fighting an answering smile. She could tell by the quirk of his mouth.

Someone else followed her down the deserted hall to the back of the house within a quarter of an hour.

He also went down the stairs. Headfirst.

"Surely there can't be more of them?" Sybil asked, peering down to watch as Pierce dragged him away.

"The last one was not Minos Society, according to Gallagher," Keir said. "But he deserves a scare for the way he tried to grab you."

"I broke his little finger," she said, shrugging.

Priya joined them, carrying a stack of printed flyers. Some of the ink had smeared in their haste, but they were legible. "It's time. I don't think your mother can fit one more person into his house."

Sybil snorted. "She could fit all of London if we'd given her one more day." She took some of the papers. "Even physics bows to my mother."

Emmeline, Matilda, and Peony also joined them, carrying the same flyers. "We're ready," Peony said. "Everyone has gathered to watch the fire eaters your mother hired."

Sybil grinned. "Ladies, let's meddle in the affairs of men."

IF SYBIL'S DOWRY of forty thousand pounds was enough to throw all of Society into an uproar, this was enough to shake them to the core.

After the applause for the fire eater had faded, the Spinster Society floated through the masked, bejeweled crowd handing out flyers.

At her mother's signal, a spangled net released flowers from the ceiling—and more flyers.

Justice snowed down.

If the Minos Society did not wish to be named, the Spinsters would name them.

If they wanted to hide, the Spinsters would light torches in every dark corner of Mayfair.

The heiresses on the Minos initiation list had already been warned. Now it came to everyone else—especially as some of those families were complicit.

The Spinsters intended there be nowhere at all left to hide.

If Minos burned down their house, they would burn down Mayfair.

The confused silence turned to gasps of outrage, muttered curses. The names of the guilty passed from mouth to ear, like a lit fuse.

The men who had attacked them, who had planned to attack other women, were safely restrained below stairs waiting for Runners and magistrates and army men, already summoned.

It was done.

Sybil surreptitiously slipped backward through the open door onto the balcony, to finally catch her breath. She had been using it as an excuse to leave all evening, but she had not actually taken a full breath since the ball started. Since last night. An irate father passed between her and Keir, shouting for his carriage and his solicitor. Keir stepped around him, his eyes never leaving Sybil.

But it was too late.

$$\sim\!\!\infty\!\!\sim$$

CHAPTER TWENTY-FIVE

I T HAPPENED TOO fast.

One moment Sybil was enjoying the commotion of the ball, the quiet of the balcony at her back, and the next something sharp pieced her side, through her stays. A familiar voice hissed in her ear. "You've ruined *everything*."

She froze. "*Victor?*"

"Why couldn't you leave well enough alone?"

Keir was already filling the doorway, cold, lethal rage simmering in his green eyes. "Get away from her, Bailey."

"No." Victor kept talking to her, the knifepoint unwavering. She would not be able to move fast enough, could not strike down at his kneecap or back with her elbow without first being gutted. Her pulse pounded hard in her ears, in her throat. "You owe me, Sybil," he continued. "You've ruined it all—the least you could do is give me your dowry."

"I'm not marrying you," she scoffed. She knew Priya would have used a sharp, rational tone. Sybil found she did not have one in her at the moment.

"You should have left us alone."

"You should have left *us* alone," she corrected him, now annoyed as well as frightened.

The dagger bit a little deeper, just enough to bring blood to the surface, welling through the fabric of her gown.

"Bailey." Keir had never sounded so arctic and vicious. So terrifying. Even Victor swallowed hard. "You're cornered. You may as well stop while you have a chance at keeping all of your limbs intact."

"I can't," Victor said. "It's too late for that. And it's all your fault, Sybil. You and those dammed Spinsters. We had to do something." He did not sound frantic or unwell. Only resolute, utterly focused. Unfortunately. "You shot Grant and scared some of the others." Now he sounded disgusted. "It's unraveling."

Some of the other pieces of the puzzle clicked.

"Lord Grant was never in charge, was he? You were Minos." He was the member who had moved quietly through the shock after the shooting. He was the one who had stabbed that man. Everything else was misdirection. Clever.

Irritating, but clever.

"And *you* were Singleton. It took me some time to figure that one out. Did you know that Portsmouth was my distant cousin?"

"He was?" Sybil frowned. "What has that to do with any-thing?"

"I was to inherit until *your lot* found him out and the title was forfeited."

"He was a murderer."

"I *needed* the estate."

Sybil rolled her eyes, even with a knife too close to her kidney. "I am sure we shall all weep ourselves to sleep over your misfortune." She struggled a little, testing his grip. She yelped at the pain in her side. He was stronger than he appeared.

"Sybil," Keir said. Whatever he could see in Victor's expression that she could not at her angle had him going very still.

"Victor, this is fruitless. You can't marry me for my dowry." And dump her body in the Thames afterward, no doubt.

"Just shut up and let me think."

"You're out of options," Keir said with quiet, pointed wrath. "I married her just this morning," he added.

Victor frowned. "You're lying."

He wasn't. Their wedding had taken place in Priya's greenhouse along the lemon trees and the lilacs, attended by their families and the Spinsters. They served plum cake afterward. It was small, simple. Perfect.

The honeymoon, however, was off to a dramatic start.

"You threatened a woman, Bailey," Keir snapped. "And a marchioness." There were penalties for threatening the peerage. "Worse, you threatened *my wife*."

Victor was taken aback at the hard edge in the most stoic marquess. She felt it in the tremble of the dagger. "I let her go and you let *me* go. Or else I stab her now and get revenge if nothing else."

A faint noise came from the shadows of the balcony, somewhere behind an urn of forsythia branches. Victor tensed, glancing toward it.

It was all it took.

One moment for everything to change.

Keir surged forward as Sybil made herself go limp. Unbalanced, Victor tried to steady her, which was an impossible feat with Keir snatching her away at the same time. He tucked her behind his body while plowing his enormous fist in Victor's face. There was a loud crack and a howl of pain. He staggered back, holding his nose, blood pooling between his fingers.

Keir turned to Sybil, ripping off his cravat and pressing it to her puncture wound. "You're hurt."

"I'm fine."

Victor snarled and lunged, dagger still in his grip.

He never reached them.

Sophie flew out from behind the urn of yellow flowers and punched him right on his already broken nose. His head snapped and he hit the railing.

"That's more than enough," Keir said. A jab to Victor's stomach sent him over the railing. There was a thump, a groan. Keir looked over the side. "He's not dead," he grumbled, clearly put out.

Had she ever really thought Keir was indifferent to her? Cared for nothing but his estate and his duties? It seemed improbable to her now. Anyone with eyeballs could see that he was a mess of feelings and fears and love. For *her*.

She threw herself into his arms, hugging him tightly.

"Here now." He sounded vaguely alarmed. "You're all right."

"I know."

They turned to Sophie, who was cradling her sore hand and beaming. "I snuck in," she said, defiantly.

"I'm so glad I have spent so much money on chaperones," Keir muttered. "Where did you learn to plant a facer like that?"

"Sybil taught me." She hovered, still unsure if she would be scolded.

"I taught you to use the heel of your hand," Sybil said. "But thank you, Sophie."

Keir paused, then sighed. Then he pulled his sister into a hug. Her eyes widened, softened. "My hand hurts," she muttered into his arm.

"We'll get you some ice. And a doctor for Sybil."

Sybil waved that off. "I don't need a doctor."

Both Montgomery siblings turned hard green gazes on her at the same time. She nearly took a prudent step back. "You are seeing a doctor," they declared in unison.

She raised her hands placatingly. "What do we do about Victor?"

"He's not going anywhere with that broken leg."

"*You broke his leg?*"

"The stone pathway broke his leg." He shrugged. So did Sophie. The Montgomery ruthlessness was clearly an inherited business. "Gallagher will see to him."

"And the doctor," Sybil insisted.

Keir was decidedly disgruntled at that. "Fine. But if he so much as looks in your direction again, I'm breaking the other leg."

"That seems fair."

Sophie blinked. "What happened to my staid big brother?"

"It was all a sham," Sybil whispered. "Don't feel bad—he even fooled himself for a while."

Keir's arm was at her waist before she even heard him move, and he scooped her up into his arms. "Not this again," she muttered, but the effect was ruined when she snuggled into his chest. "I can walk. I'm not even bleeding anymore."

"You're going to sit by the fire until someone can look at that cut." His jaw clenched, unclenched. She smoothed her fingertips over it.

"I'm fine."

"You are perfect."

She shook her head. "Hardly."

"Perfect for *me*." He kissed her gently, thoroughly. "Don't scare me like that again."

"I'll try not to."

"Are you ready to come home with me?"

"Yes, Keir. Let's go home."

He kissed her again. And again.

Until they realized they had crossed back into the pandemonium of the ballroom. But even a hundred flyers and the bad deeds of bad men were not enough to distract from the Marquess Blackburn carrying the orphan girl from Seven Dials.

And kissing her.

A lot.

A hush fell as heads turned, eyes widened. Whispers swelled almost immediately.

"Oh dear, most unseemly of us." Sybil grinned.

"You are definitely a bad influence," Keir murmured. "I look forward to scandalizing the *ton* on a regular basis."

"Raise your glasses to my daughter, Sybil Taunton, the guest of honor," her father called out, a glass of champagne in his hand.

Amandine smiled smugly, motioning for the footmen. A cloud of white butterflies flew from gold birdcages that had been draped in silver silk. "Also, as of this morning, the Marchioness

Blackburn!"

Every eye in the room blinked at Sybil, maskless, her hair falling from its pins, her gown torn at the hem and stained with blood.

EPILOGUE

MARCHIONESS BLACKBURN'S SCHOOL for Young Ladies was the premiere finishing school in Mayfair.

Even when it did not officially exist.

There was an extensive waiting list. Those who could afford tuition paid exorbitantly, in order to sponsor those who could not.

As Sybil was no longer a spinster, and was a marchioness to boot, fading into the background had become a little more difficult. She would always be a Spinster, always a member of the Society—but her work looked different now. It had to. She had an annoying number of social calls and invitations to dodge. Or use to her students' benefit.

Emmeline and Matilda stayed on with Priya. Clara, once a Spinster and now living at the seaside with her captain of a husband, had begun training chaperones.

Not the usual kind, naturally.

These chaperones knew the rules of Polite Society, of course. Clara had always been good at that sort of thing. But they also knew how to spot unsavory suitors. And slip laudanum in their tea.

Kitty continued to run her bookshop with her sister, who kept late hours when Kitty could not. Devil continued to send a veritable army to protect them both, but he had learned to be subtle about it. It was generally bad for business when one stopped in for a naughty book and was met with hulking military men of a dubious nature. And if there was one thing Kitty would not tolerate, it was something interfering with her bookshop business.

Peony split her time between Spinster House and the school.

Sybil was quite certain that, given a few years, the Spinster Society could take over London. England.

For now, she had two new students currently in the back garden with her three original students, Sophie, Jane, and Margaret. More applied every day, some with their parents' approval, many without.

The Marchioness Blackburn had become very good at hosting tea parties.

If those tea parties usually involved target practice with knives, stabbing with hatpins, or tips on how to spot a fortune hunter from a mile away, that was nobody's business.

And anyway, Peony's brutal obstacle courses had more in common with the social obstacle courses of Mayfair than most people realized. The back garden was for something in between tea and target practice.

An old carriage waited under the shade of an oak tree. The paint was peeling and one of the windows was cracked, but it was otherwise sound. The door was open, steps leading up. It looked like any other carriage. In fact, one of their new students nodded at it. "My governess used to make me practice climbing into a carriage without flashing my ankles. Is that what we are doing today?"

Jane smiled. "Not exactly." Her cheeks were no longer red with nerves but now freckled with the sun. Her mother did not approve. Jane had discovered that she did not mind half as much as she had feared.

One of the footmen emerged from the shadows.

"I hope at least one of you noticed him there," Sybil said. The girls paused to stare at him, then at her.

Peony, who had sauntered in from behind a hedge, sighed. "No one even saw me back there, so I am not hopeful."

"Who wants to go first?" Sybil asked.

No one volunteered, though Sophie, who had been through this course before, smirked.

"No one?" Sybil nodded to Lady Mary. She was very slight, with a delicate posture and a twenty-thousand-pound inheritance. She would need to know this. Posthaste. "Lady Mary."

Mary hesitated, then marched forward with admirable determination. She knew only enough to know that something was afoot. That was good. Sybil taught her girls not only to be aware of their surroundings, but to know that everything could change without warning.

For instance, the footman was exceedingly dashing.

Ridiculously dashing. Distractingly so.

Being distracted was the first mistake.

Mary put her gloved fingers on his arm with a polite nod and peeked into the carriage.

Good.

But not quite good enough.

In the blink of an eye—or rather, a wink from a dashing gentleman—Mary was shoved onto the carriage and the door slammed shut. And locked.

"Hello?" She called out. "Lady Blackburn?"

Sybil waited.

Mary tried the handle. Pounded on the door. "Hello?"

"You've been abducted, Lady Mary," Sybil called out. "And you are now, regrettably, on your way to Gretna Green with a man who is quite enamored of your twenty thousand pounds. Now what do you do?"

Mary screamed.

It was much louder than expected. Sybil and Peony exchanged an approving nod.

"Good," Peony said. "But you'll have to do better than that."

"Sir!" Mary shouted through the cracked window. "I will pay

you double what he is paying you to release me."

Sybil beamed. "Oh, I do like you, Lady Mary. Well done! What else?"

The footman yanked open the door and Mary nearly tumbled out. She found her balance, but too late. He already had her. Again.

She cursed. Clawed. Tried to bite him.

Peony nodded at him, and he tossed the girl into the grass.

She landed on her back, wind knocked out of her, hair falling from its pins. Sybil leaned over to look down at her. "First lesson: a helping hand into a gentleman's carriage could turn into an abduction by a fortune hunter heading to Gretna Green." She glanced at the others. The new students gaped back. "There *are* steps to take should that occur. Messages to leave at inns along the Great North Road and so forth. We'll get to that. But the first step is not to be taken. Who's next?"

"Don't worry," Margaret added, helping Mary to her feet. "It gets easier. And later we get to punch a dummy filled with straw. It's very cathartic."

"Try it again with a flour sack over her head," Sybil said.

Mary gulped.

Seeing as everything was well in hand, Sybil went back to the house. She had a ridiculous list of invitations to decline. Behind her, the girls shouted encouragement at the next effort to escape the carriage. It was the best sound in the world. And the best weapon.

The house was bright and not quite tidy. It was home as much as Montgomery House was home, now that it had been stripped of every drapery and gold tassel and delicate teacup. The ornate atrocity of a clock was sold and the funds used to furnish her school.

Strong hands pulled her abruptly into one of the closets where they stored sharpened hatpins and parasols with fortified handles. The door shut firmly behind her. She knew those hands, the curve of that mouth against her neck, even in the darkness.

"Is this a test?" she teased. Peony enjoyed springing situations on her students almost as much as she enjoyed springing them on Sybil herself.

Keir's only answer was a gentle nip at the side of her throat, and she leaned into him, already tingling with need. She gripped his arms, adoring the bulk of muscle shifting under her touch, the heat of his body already warming her. "What are you doing here?" she murmured on a gasp when he dragged his teeth up to her earlobe. "Shouldn't you be at home? Doing whatever it is that marquesses do?"

"You left too early this morning, and it's been very quiet over there. Very well mannered," he complained. "I don't care for it at all." He backed her against the wall, kissing her deeply. "And this *is* what a marquess does. He makes love to his wife."

"How very"—she whimpered when he used his boot to nudge her legs wider—"proper of you."

"I take my duties very seriously."

"Thank God."

The kiss seared her even after all these months. Still. Always.

His mouth was clever and demanding and he was desperate for her, almost as desperate as she was for him. She nipped at his bottom lip, at his tongue, until he pressed against her, pulling her knee up to better rock into the cradle of her thighs. She gasped at the friction, the perfect pressure.

When there was a sound from the hallway, Keir turned the key in the lock without moving his attention away from her. He gripped the inside of her thigh under her skirts, trailing up to slide his fingers through her wet heat. Her gasp turned into a whimper. Need pulsed through her, her bud already swollen and throbbing.

"Shh," he scolded in her ear. "You need to be quiet, my little scoundrel."

Her eyes twinkled with mischief. "You first, Lord Blackburn."

She finally managed to fumble his buttons open so she could feel the silky hardness of him jutting into her palm. He slipped his fingers inside her, curling for the angle she loved so much. It was a contest, a competition to see who could become undone first.

The very best kind of rivalry.

When he groaned, she slapped her hand over his mouth.

"Have you seen the marchioness?" one of the maids said from the other side of the door.

"No, but I'm sure she's about somewhere. I saw the marquess just now."

"Dear God, you're new, so I'll warn you not to go inside any closed rooms without knocking first." A pause. "Even a closet."

Sybil and Keir grinned at each other as he thrust into her, sliding her back up against the wall, pinning her with his body. She bit into his shoulder to keep from crying out, his mouth still against her palm. She clung to him as each stroke brought her closer and closer to release. He reached down between them, stroking her bud, his big body easily holding her up. He waited until she was fluttering around him, squeezing him with the waves of her pleasure before giving in. They came together, panting, holding tight.

Keir smiled down at her. "Scoundrel," he murmured fondly.

"You know how they are," the housemaid continued as she crossed on the other side of the door. "It's sweet, really."

"He doesn't much act like a marquess, does he?"

Sybil kissed Keir softly, their panting breaths mingling, her legs still wrapped right around his waist. "And thank God for that."

About the Author

Alyxandra Harvey lives in an old stone house with her husband, multiple dogs, and a few resident ghosts who are allowed to stay as long as they keep company manners. She likes chai lattes, tattoos, and books. Sometimes fueled by literary rage.

Author of The Drake Chronicles, The Witches of London, Haunting Violet, Red, Love Me Love Me Not.

Twitter: AlyxandraH
Instagram: alyxandraharveyauthor